WALDO: A YOUNG WYOMING COWBOY

Good times & great dreams

J. C. Cantle

WALDO: A YOUNG WYOMING COWBOY

By

J.C. Cantle

HOMESTEAD PUBLISHING
Moose, Wyoming

DEDICATION

This book is dedicated to Cooper G., who at the age of
five revealed a great love for the cowboy and speared my
interest in writing the story of Waldo.
To my granddaughter Lindsey Rose and to the memory
of my friend Jim Chambers, cowboy rancher, story teller
and an all around good man.

ISBN 0-943972-27-2
Library of Congress Catalog Card Number 93-80773
Printed in the United States of America
on recycled, acid free paper.

Cover credit—Indian blanket
Cat. #9315. Navajo textile, Classic period. Douglas Kahn, photographer. School
of American Research Collections in Museum of New Mexico, Santa Fe.

Published by
HOMESTEAD PUBLISHING
Box 193, Moose, Wyoming 83012

TABLE OF CONTENTS

The west is dead my friend, but writers hold the seed and what they sow will live and grow again to those who read.
Charles M. Russell, 1917

Chapter 1

WALDO SPARKS was fourteen years old in 1899. He had been orphaned two years earlier, when his mother died of the cough. And just three years before that, nine-year-old Waldo's blue-green eyes had widened in horror as the squealing, bucking bronco reared and toppled backward, crushing Jed Sparks' lungs beneath the saddlehorn. Waldo's father had died with his boots on.

Since his mother's death, Waldo had been living with his aunt and uncle—Frank and Betty Korn—on their K Bar Ranch, east of the Medicine Bow River in Wyoming. The fifty-odd square miles of ranch was originally homesteaded a few years before Wyoming became a state.

Waldo was a fair-haired boy, already 5'4" tall and lean built. Before moving to Wyoming, he had lived with his mother in Coldwater, Kansas, not far from the Oklahoma border. Kansas was far different from Wyoming; the summers were hot and humid, and tornadoes were always a threat to man, beast and property.

Waldo came by train from Wichita, Kansas to Cheyenne, Wyoming, then by stagecoach over the Sherman Mountains to Laramie. He then traveled the remaining 60 miles to the town of Elk Mountain on a wagon pulled by four mules and loaded with goods for

the town of Rawlins. The stage to Rawlins was broken down and the blacksmith couldn't get it fixed for a couple of days, so Waldo got a ride to Elk Mountain, the nearest town to the K Bar Ranch. Waldo's ride with the teamster was tiresome, bumpy and very dusty. He used his jacket as a cushion to sit on, but it didn't help soften the ride much. The occasional whack of the teamster's whip only made the mules move faster for a minute before returning to the same slow pace.

The heavy-set teamster was not one for conversation; he preferred chewing tobacco and spitting. Tobacco juice was dried to his long ill-kept beard, and the man smelled worse than the team.

Waldo slapped his neck repeatedly, killing the biting flies. Each time he did, the driver would look at him sideways and grunt. When they reached Elk Mountain, Waldo thanked the driver for the lift and, at the same time, was glad to be out of the wagon.

This spring, Waldo was to go on round-up and branding with the cowboys of the K Bar and the Double X ranches. The ranches worked together when there was a big job to be done. Waldo was a good rider, and his Uncle Frank had given him a two-year-old buckskin mare, fourteen hands tall.

Waldo named the mare "Buck" for lack of a better idea at the time. Buck had a black mane and tail, and she was a light-tanned deerskin color, with four black hooves and knee-high black socks. With the help and watchful eye of one of the cowboys, D.J. Faiths, Waldo had gently broken Buck to ride. D.J. had been working on the K Bar for six years now, and he was not only a good roper but also a natural around horses.

D.J. was a lanky man of average height, with a straight back. His moustache was full and it sometimes looked like it needed a good trimming. He had a habit of putting his right hand behind him, in the waistband of his pants, when he was standing around talking.

Waldo's job during branding was to help the cook by bringing in firewood and keeping the fires hot when the branding irons—all twenty-six irons, including ten K Bar and fourteen Double X's, plus two running irons used to clean up any bad marks—were to be heated.

The cook's name was Charlie Stronghorse. He was an old half-breed Indian, whose mother had been sold to the Comanches by some Comancheros. Charlie was from Oklahoma or Texas, nobody really knew. He left the reservation and never went back. The man had been around white people for so long now that he talked and sounded like a white man. Charlie had been a cowboy until he had been shot in the left leg, which never mended right. He limped badly and had a rough time climbing into the chuckwagon seat, but he had an impossible time getting a foot up into the stirrup, so he had become the cook. He knew how to make coffee, burn meat, make sourdough biscuits light as a feather and take the small stones out of the pinto beans before he made chili.

While the cowboys and wagons were on the move, Waldo rode in the chuckwagon next to Charlie, with Buck on a lead rope, tied to an O-ring on the back of the wagon. When camp was made that night, it was Waldo's job to find firewood wherever he could on the prairie. Bits of dried, dead sagebrush or willow—even dried cow dung—would burn nicely and make a hot fire. The firewood suspended by chains under the wagon was not to be used for cooking. It was all good lodgepole pine and aspen for the branding fires and was on hand just in case the area of the cow camp had

little wood to burn. An extremely hot fire was needed to get the branding irons red hot. There were three wagons on this round-up, including two bedroll and tent wagons, plus the chuckwagon that hauled the food, cook pots, and drinking water. When the cow camp was made for good, the tents went up and the wagon canvases were stretched out to the backs of the wagons by rope and poles, as protection from the sun and the rain. The day began before first light, with the wranglers going out and driving the thirty-four head of horses back to camp. Some of the horses wore bells so the cowboys could find them in the dark morning hours. Some of the others had been hobbled to keep them from going too far. Horses were hobbled by their front legs so that they couldn't run off but still were able to move around to eat.

When the horses reached the outskirts of the cow camp, they were tied to a long picket line, forming a string of horses called the remuda. From this remuda, the cowboys picked out their mounts for the day or half-day based on how hard the animal had to work. At noon, the cowboys would change horses for a fresh mount.

In the evening, when the branding irons were left to cool, Waldo had a little time to himself—that was, if Charlie didn't need him to do the dishes. He would quickly rope Buck and saddle her with an old high-back, A-forked, center-fire California saddle, which had belonged to his Uncle Frank. The strings had been eaten by mice one winter, and the cantle was worn to the rawhide tree in spots. The horn had long ago lost its leather and the iron was exposed, but the sheepskin under the skirts was still in good shape. It had a new horse-hair cinch that D.J. had braided while in a line shack last winter and then had given to Waldo for Christ-

mas. When Buck was saddled and the rawhide bosal and hackamore with the horsehair reins were on, Waldo whistled for Cheyenne, the one and only dog on the branding roundup.

Uncle Frank got the dog some years back, at a blacksmith's and livery in Cheyenne. At the time, the male dog was the largest in a litter of seven puppies. Frank Korn had fallen in love with this mutt, which had big feet and one blue eye, known as a "Sioux eye." Frank named the dog after the city in which it had been born. The pup rode back to the K Bar, sleeping most of the trip under the wagon seat. When Waldo arrived at the K Bar Ranch a few years later, he and Cheyenne became close friends.

Waldo mounted Buck and, with Cheyenne in the lead, took off to see the cow herd feeding and watering at the edge of the Medicine Bow River. Most of the young calves were suckling their evening meal while their mothers licked the calves' new burned-in brands. These brands soon would scab over, and the scabs eventually would fall off, leaving a smooth scar. As each calf grew, so would the size of the brand mark. The scar of the brand would cover over with new hair, but it would grow back in a different direction than it should so that a cowboy would almost always be able to see the brand and know to what ranch the cow belonged.

Sitting on Buck's back, Waldo watched the sunset with its great and beautiful colors. As it became darker, Waldo could see the stars come out. He was so glad to be alive; he breathed in deeply, smelling the sage and distant wood smoke. Giving Buck a pat on the neck and calling the dog, Waldo then rode back to the cow camp, where his warm bedroll awaited. With Cheyenne sleeping next to him, Waldo's night was filled with happy dreams of becoming a cowboy.

Chapter 2

WALDO WOKE to the sound of the horse bells, as the wranglers and nighthawks—the night cowboys who kept watch on the herd—brought the team into camp. The smell of coffee and smoke signaled Waldo to get up quickly. He put on his shoes, as he didn't own a pair of cowboy boots yet. Uncle Frank told him he'd get him some when his feet stopped growing. Waldo rolled up his bedroll and put on his coat and hat. The air was cold, and he could see his breath as puffs of steam when he exhaled.

Most of the cowboys of the K Bar and Double X ranches were drinking coffee, and some were rolling smokes, "coffin nails," as they were known. Others were dishing up platefuls of biscuits and gravy that had been fried up with pieces of salt pork. Waldo dished up his bait, or vittles, and ate quickly because he had to get the branding fire going and the irons hot.

That morning, he watched the cowboys bringing in calves roped in the herd. Once a calf was drawn close to the fire, a couple of cowboys would roll it on its side and stretch it, by pulling its back legs one way and its front legs and head the other way. This was to keep it from jumping up before it had been branded. The rider who brought the calf in would announce whether it was a K

Bar or Double X calf, so that it would receive the right brand. The ear marking and wattles were cut as another means to identify them, and the castration of calves to become steers also was taken care of. In the air was the smell of burning hair and the sound of bawling calves. The entire procedure lasted only a couple of minutes per calf, after which Waldo put the iron back into the fire to reheat.

Uncle Frank was nearby watching what was going on and keeping the tally in his notebook. As one calf was released to return to its mother and another was brought to the branding fire, Monte Higgins, trail boss for the Double X, came loping in. Monte told Frank that there was a steer with a broken leg that would have to be shot and used as camp meat. Uncle Frank told Waldo to go get Charlie, help him harness one of the teams to a wagon, and ride out to the injured steer.

"It musta broke a leg in a badger hole or somethin'," Monte said.

The wagon came upon the helpless steer just as Monte was aiming the barrel of his .44 Winchester, model 1866 yellow boy, between the steer's eyes. A shot rang out and the steer fell to the ground, dead.

Charlie and Waldo climbed off the wagon. With his sharp knife, Charlie began gutting out the steer while Waldo helped by holding the legs out of Charlie's way. When the animal was gutted and split up the middle, Charlie retrieved his Green River skinning knife from the wagon box.

"Waldo, I reckon we oughta dry this here hide out good, and then I'll show ya how to braid a reata like an ol' Mexican showed me," Charlie said as he skinned the steer. Waldo said he would

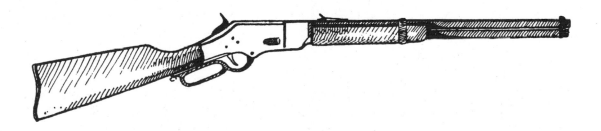

like to learn how to braid rawhide. And when the hide was stripped off the cow, rolled up and thrown in the wagon, Charlie and Waldo cut the steer into quarters so it would be easier to load.

They got back to camp at 11 a.m. After Waldo helped Charlie hang the meat in the shade of the chuckwagon, he went back to the branding fire. Charlie said they would stretch out the steer's hide later but that it was OK in the shade for now.

Charlie went and checked his dutch ovens to see if the beans, chopped onions, and salt-pork stew were all right and to put another pot of water on the fire for coffee.

Coffee was made by adding a large fistful of fresh-ground coffee beans to a two-gallon pot of boiling water. If Charlie had used any eggs that morning, an eggshell or two was added to the coffee to settle the grounds and to prevent it from tasting bitter. The dough had risen for the bread and Charlie punched it down and kneaded it again. In another dutch oven—after greasing it with lard—he made small round rolls and placed them two inches apart. With the cover on the dutch oven, Charlie allowed them to sit in the hot sun to rise again. Then he surrounded the oven with hot coals and let the whole thing bake.

At high noon, Charlie rang the triangle with the iron spoon. The ringing could be heard for miles, and the cowboys, or "waddies," as they were called, would know the chuck was ready. If they wanted their bait, it was time to ride into camp and chow down.

After the noon meal, Waldo had to help Charlie. He did up the dishes while the old Indian cook peeled potatoes and sliced onions for supper. Then they put one of the front quarters of the beef on the iron spit, and Waldo turned it slowly over the fire.

After rolling a smoke, Charlie would take Waldo's place, and Waldo again would look for firewood, as Cheyenne followed, chasing after jackrabbits along the way. Waldo had an old grass rope that he normally carried on his saddle. It was a short rope and just about shot. When he gathered up a pile of firewood, he would tie the old twelve-foot rope around it and drag it back to camp.

That afternoon, Waldo and Charlie rolled out the green hide— a raw wet hide—on the ground, with the flesh side up and the hair side down. They staked it and stretched it at the same time. Then Charlie gave Waldo an old dull knife and showed him how to scrape the hide, while he went back to turning the beef over the fire.

By the time Charlie rang the triangle for supper, Waldo had the old steer hide well-scraped, good and clean.

The next morning would be Sunday. Charlie told Waldo he was going to make sourdough "pan-ee-cakes," as he called them, for breakfast. So, on Saturday night, Charlie made a big batch of sourdough batter in an old pickle crock and set it near the heat of the fire to stay warm through the night. The sourdough starter that Charlie kept in a mason jar was given to him by Mrs. Korn.

Waldo was tired that night because he had worked hard all day, and he was glad to be in his warm bedroll with his old saddle as a pillow. He lay there listening to Cheyenne gnaw on a bone. He could hear the cowboys talking and the distant sound of a coyote, as well as some nighthawk playing his mouth harp to the cows.

He woke early Sunday morning when Cheyenne jumped over him to spot a coyote that was yapping under the light of the moon. Charlie was already mixing up the pancake batter.

Sourdough pancakes with molasses were Waldo's favorite breakfast, so he made sure his plate was loaded up good. Monte told Charlie he was the best "biscuit shooter" he had ever known.

By the next Wednesday, all the new calves and mavericks had been branded. The cow camp was broken down and the wagons were loaded. The cows were left to graze, the horse cavvy rounded up, and everyone headed back to their ranches—to the cookhouse, the bunkhouse, and a good bath in the Medicine Bow River.

Waldo had taken the dry steer hide and made sure it was packed in the chuckwagon before they left camp. When they got back to the ranch, Charlie and Waldo nailed the old hide to the sunny side of the bunkhouse with the hair side out and, once again, Waldo continued to scrape the hide, until all the hair was off. They let it dry for another week and a half. When the hide was good and dry, Charlie Stronghorse began cutting one long continuous string, a half inch wide. He started cutting on the outside of the hide and kept cutting in a circle around the hide until he ended up in the center. With Waldo's help, they doubled this length of the rawhide string by stretching it out and cutting it into two equal pieces. They doubled up the two strings and ended up with four equal lengths of string. Charlie then made four bundles of rawhide strings.

That evening, he tied the four ends of the strings to an O-ring and nailed it to the bunkhouse wall. Slowly and carefully, Charlie began braiding the four strings together, making sure the flat strings always lay in the same way, with no twists. He pulled firmly as he braided, keeping everything good and tight. Charlie let Waldo try but Waldo just couldn't get the hang of it. He suggested that Waldo practice on some scrap pieces.

Each night, they would braid two or three feet of the rope. After they had a good six feet braided, Charlie would take what was braided, choke up on the O-ring, and keep on braiding.

Charlie finally finished the forty-five feet of rawhide reata—which he thought was long enough for Waldo. Reatas were eighty feet long or longer in the California vaquero days, were made from six strings and were about a half inch thick. Charlie stretched the new reata, putting in the twist as he did. That night, he showed Waldo the art of making the rawhide honda with a Turk's head bottom. He worked on it late into the night but didn't finish it until the next night.

The following day, Charlie put the entire reata together and said: "Well, Waldo, I got 'er done and since I don't ride the herds no more, I reckon you should have it."

Waldo's eyes opened wide with excitement. "Thanks, Charlie, thanks! I thought you were making it to sell in town."

"Nope," Charlie declared, "It's yourn now."

Chapter 3

THE DAY was gray and overcast, a "hangdog" day as D.J. called it. The temperature was a few degrees cooler than it had been of late, and it looked like it might rain, or even snow. In the spring, Wyoming weather was very unpredictable.

Despite the weather, however, Waldo was happy. He had a new stiff reata and, this morning, he was planning to soften it with tallow from the same steer whose hide was used to make it. D.J. said that it would work well in making the reata more pliable, though bear fat, when available, was the best dressing for rawhide and leather.

First, Waldo had his chores to do—feed the chickens, check for eggs in the barn, and split and stack the cooking firewood in the old woodbox in the kitchen. The Monarch wood cooking stove had a water tank next to it, so hot water was always available to Mrs Korn. Charlie cooked when the men were in the field on roundup or on a cattle drive, but Mrs. Korn did the cooking at the ranch.

Mrs. Korn's first name was Betty, but Waldo called her "Auntie." She always wanted an ample supply of split aspen or cottonwood because it would burn fast and hot, perfect for cooking. Aunt Betty was a very good cook, but she loved to bake even more. She had beautiful soft brown hair, hazel eyes, and was heavy

set, but not fat. It seemed to Waldo that she wore her apron all the time.

When Charlie wasn't working as a cook, he would do odd jobs around the ranch, mending corrals, butchering, or cutting firewood. And he usually would be the one to drive the wagon into the town of Elk Mountain for supplies—at least once a month. Waldo was his helper.

D.J. and the other cowboys would do the cruising after the cows and the necessary breaking of the horses to be ridden, as well as other ranch work. Cruising was when a cowboy rode the open range, keeping an eye on the cows' welfare. When Waldo had completed his chores, he checked with Charlie to see if there was anything he could do to help. Charlie was just greasing the wagon hubs and axles, so Waldo went to Uncle Frank, but Uncle Frank was busy with paperwork and said that Waldo could cruise the Wagonhound Creek area in the afternoon. He also told Waldo to take his 1873 Winchester and a box of .45-caliber ammo. The carbine was only 38½ inches long and weighed just over seven pounds. Waldo would carry this carbine whenever he was riding out on his own. Uncle Frank thought it was a safer gun for Waldo than a belly gun. Uncle Frank always had a handgun and holster at his side, and he didn't like parting with his Remington single action .45. When Waldo used the carbine, the saddle gun was strapped to the saddle in a scabbard.

Waldo went to the springhouse and got some tallow from an old burlap bag hanging next to the salted slabs of bacon. He spent the rest of the morning working the tallow into the reata. When he got it as pliable as he wanted it, he went out to the corral. There he practiced roping the pegging post, and later roping the goats. Cheyenne was watching but kept his distance, as he wasn't interested in getting roped.

At about noon, Chic Mitchell, riding his bald-faced bay horse, rode up behind Waldo and watched.

"Looks like you're getting the hang of it, Waldo," Chic said. Waldo turned, saw Chic and replied with a "Howdy Chic!"

Chic Mitchell was a tall Texican from Del Rio, near the Tex-Mex border. He had worked the spread, or rancho as it was known there, called the Diamond Bench. Chic could speak Spanish and also loved playing cards, poker mostly. When he was in town, he would always have a bit too much snake juice and would become half-shot. Chic once said that he had been born the same year that Abraham Lincoln was assassinated and the Civil War ended. That was 1865, which made him 34 years old. He had a handle-bar mustache, always wore his vest, leather cuffs, and a flat-topped hat. His chaps were shotgun-style, with a series of conchos and fringe down the sides of the legs.

Chic started working on the K Bar Ranch the same year that Waldo arrived there. "Never lose a stirrup and never waste a loop" was his most often-used expression. He was an excellent roper.

Chic stepped out of the saddle and grabbed his lasso. "Waldo," he said, "let me show you some throws you can practice." He showed Waldo how to shake out a good loop, how to side cast, and how to execute the Hoolihan throw.

After noon chuck, Waldo saddled Buck and tied on his reata and carbine with scabbard. They rode off, again with Cheyenne in the lead.

"Keep your heels down in the stirrups when you ride!," Chic

4-A

yelled to Waldo. Waldo waved, set his heels down, and loped east toward Wagonhound Creek.

He had only been out for half an hour when it began raining. Waldo untied his slicker from the cantle and put on his "fish." Slickers were called fish because the cowboys' slickers had labels in them that read, "Towers Fish Brand Pommel Slicker, made in Boston." Originally yellow, the color aged with use to a copper tone. The fish were made of stiff oil cloth.

By now, there was a hard drizzle of rain coming down and the ground was getting very muddy. Waldo rode at a walk as they headed north along Wagonhound Creek. Buck shook the water off her head and Cheyenne trotted with his tail between his legs. Waldo skirted a large pond-like area that the creek ran through and stayed on higher ground, away from the white alkaline and the greasy bentonite ground. He could see cows up ahead, and heard one bawling and another mooing back. The closer Waldo got, the better view he got of the cattle. One old cow was looking out in the pond and calling to a calf stuck in the bentonite mud clear up to its neck. As Waldo got closer, he got his reata coil in his left hand and got the loop shaken out with his right hand and swung it over his head. He let the full loop cast 30 feet and caught the calf by the neck. He took a couple of wraps around the saddle horn (dallying), turned Buck uphill and jerked the poor calf out of the gumbo. Once the calf was out, Waldo dismounted, ran over to the calf, wrestled it to the ground and took the reata off the calf. The calf jumped up and ran to its mother, as Waldo coiled his reata up and climbed back into the saddle. He still had five more miles of range to cruise before he could head back to the ranch.

The drizzle finally stopped and the sun came out. Waldo had now reached a place called Third Sand, where he looked over all the cattle in the area.

Cows have a way of setting up a baby-sitting arrangement among themselves. When the calves lay down to nap, one cow stays close by, keeping an eye out while the others graze on ahead. But today the baby sitter was about to have some trouble. In the sage and tall bunch grass, two dark figures were stalking an unsuspecting calf. Suddenly a shot rang out and a bullet kicked up rocks and mud in the face of one of the wolves. The two wolves turned in unison and ran hell-bent for leather, as Waldo pulled the lever on the Winchester and got off two more shots. Though he had not hit the wolves, Waldo had kicked up quite a storm of mud and rocks and the wolves wouldn't return, at least not that day.

When Waldo reached the ranch, it was late and the men had already eaten, but Uncle Frank, D.J. and Chic hadn't unsaddled their horses yet. As this was the first time Waldo had gone cruising alone, Frank Korn had told them that if Waldo didn't show up soon they'd go looking for him. When Waldo appeared at the ranch, everyone was glad to see him. He told them about the stuck calf and the two wolves. Uncle Frank complimented him on a job well done, and Chic added: "I'll have to teach you how to rope a steer now, since you now know how to catch a calf."

The next day, Waldo was to go with Charlie to Elk Mountain. They were to get the mail, flour, coal for the forge, a keg of nails and enough rough-sawn lumber for a new barn door.

The trip to Elk Mountain was a bit muddy in a few places. They arrived there in the late morning. The town was small, only seven buildings. The largest was the log Mercantile store, which was also the post office and the lumber dealer. In addition, the town included the blacksmith shop, livery and wheelwright—housed in a large barn—plus four houses and a small schoolhouse. The town had no jail, saloon, bank or church, so it was free of what the cowboys called badgers, wolves and coyotes. Main Street—the only street—was somewhat muddy but was drying up fast. The only boardwalk was in front of the Merc. Mr. Rasmussen, the store's proprietor, was sweeping the dried mud off the walk.

"Gud mornin' Charlie, Valdo," he called out as their wagon and team pulled up to the front of the Merc.

"Morning!," they called back.

"Vhat you needin' today?," he asked.

"Lumber and nails," Charlie said. "And some flour and any mail ya got fur da ranch. Also a box of .41-caliber ammo and two boxes of .44-cal."

Waldo looked at Charlie with a questioning look. Charlie told Waldo that the .41s were for himself and the .44s were for D.J. The last time they'd been in town was six weeks ago.

"For de nails and lumber, pull de vagon around back, and come in for the rest," Rasmussen told them.

Mr. Rasmussen was a Danish who had been in America since he was a young man, but he still talked with a bit of an accent. After the wagon was loaded, Charlie and Waldo went into the Merc.

"Here's the mail, flour and ammo, Charlie. Anything else?"

"Yeah," Charlie said. "Frank Korn wants any of the Laramie or Cheyenne papers ya got."

Rasmussen pulled out four old newspapers, three from Laramie and one *Cheyenne Sun*, all of them four weeks old. "Any-

thing else?," Rasmussen asked. "You can have the papers; it's mostly old news now."

"Thanks," Charlie said. "And we might as well have a couple of sodies too."

The coal had to be picked up from the blacksmith, so Charlie and Waldo drove the team and wagon over to Ox's. Ox was the blacksmith's nickname, because of his size. He was not too tall but was built like an ox, with wide shoulders and large muscular arms.

"What can I do for you gents?," Ox asked.

"Need some coal," Waldo said.

Ox took them to the back of the livery and retrieved a burlap bag full of coal. At the forge was an older Mexican heating a piece of iron white hot

"This here is my new helper, Alfonso Garcia, best spur and bit maker I've seen," Ox said.

"Howdy!," Waldo and Charlie shot back. Alfonso nodded his head and said "Buenos dias, señors," and went on working.

"He don't speak much English," Ox said. "He's from Tularosa, New Mexico. Come, and I'll show you some of his handy work." Ox pulled out six sets of spurs and five bits that Alfonso had made.

"Wow!," Waldo exclaimed, "He does good work."

"If I was still ridin'," Charlie added, "I'd have him make me some spurs."

"They're a buck and a half or three bucks 'pending on how much Mexican silver is on them," Ox responded.

They bid "Adios," to Alfonso, who returned with an "Adios, amigos."

As they headed out of town, Charlie kidded, "Any mail for me?"

"No, two for Uncle Frank, and one for D.J. and that's it."

Waldo was attempting to read the *Cheyenne Sun,* and Charlie asked, "Anything worthwhile in that paper?"

"Hard to say," Waldo answered. "I can hardly read it with the wagon bouncing around."

"But there is an article on President McKinley's health," he continued. "It don't look good. And on page two, the Wyoming Stock Growers Association is back to fighting the Johnson County War all over again. It's rumored that the big ranches around Casper and Buffalo hired a man called Tom Horn as a cattle detective to catch rustlers. Says he's from Arizona and was instrumental in capturing Geronimo."

"Charlie!" Waldo announced, "Here's an ad in the Laramie paper saying that there's going to be a big horse sale. The Army is getting rid of some of their horses at this sale too. Uncle Frank might be interested in that."

Chapter 4

FRANK KORN read the ad in the *Laramie Republican-Boomerang* newspaper about the horse sale. (The *Boomerang* was one of the first newspapers in Laramie and was named after the editor's pet mule.) After some thought, he decided that it might be worth looking into.

The sale was to take place thirty days from the date the ad appeared in the newspaper. The distance to Laramie was a little under seventy miles, which meant it would take about three and a half days to get there if they took their time riding at twenty miles a day.

Frank decided to leave as soon as possible because the sale was the coming weekend. He said he would take Chic and Waldo with him to aid in bringing back any horses he might buy. D.J. and Charlie could take care of things while they were gone.

The following morning, the three were on their way to Laramie. They took with them a few cooking utensils, coffee and coffee pot, salt pork, beans and jerky, all of which Betty Korn packed into a flour sack and Waldo tied to his saddle. Each also wrapped their blankets in their fish and tied them to the saddle cantles.

Waldo had a hard time getting Cheyenne to stay behind voluntarily, so Charlie had to tie the dog up for the day.

By noon, the threesome was almost to Rock Creek, but Frank wanted to get to Duncan Creek before they stopped for the night. If they made it that far without trouble on the first day, it might take only three days to get to Laramie, at an easy ride and without wearing out the horses.

They reached Duncan Creek just after dark, and made a dry camp—a camp without a fire—for the night because no one wanted to bother cooking. After unsaddling and hobbling the horses, the three men ate jerky, drank water out of the canteen, and then slept on the hard ground.

In the morning, Chic woke first and decided to make a fire and get some coffee going. Breakfast was coffee and a chunk of dried salt pork. Waldo wished Charlie was along with the chuckwagon so they could have a better breakfast. The horses were saddled and the riders headed east just as daylight was appearing over the hills.

The second day's ride was hot; the sun beat down with its full force, and there was not even a slight breeze. They saw a lot of antelope and some of the Morgan and Quealy Ranch cows grazing. That night, they camped on a hill some two hundred yards from Laramie Creek, so the mosquitoes wouldn't be so bad if a breeze came up during the night.

This time, they made a small fire and ate a bean and coffee supper. They kept the fire going and added some green sage so the smoke would help keep some of the bugs away.

Before Waldo knew it, it was morning again and Uncle Frank was getting the fire going. Waldo didn't want to get up just yet, as he was still dead tired, but he had to pee so bad that there was no way he could stay wrapped in his blanket any longer.

Today, they didn't start out until 5:30 a.m., and it was daylight.

Waldo was glad to hear Uncle Frank say that tonight they'd be eating dinner in a restaurant and sleeping in a bed. And as they rode that day, Waldo's mind was full of questions.

"Uncle Frank," Waldo asked, "What does Wyoming mean?"

"It's an Indian word meaning 'end of the plains,' but it's not Arapahoe, Shoshoni or Sioux, as far as I know."

Wyoming is Delaware Indian signifying the end, plains, therefore, the end of the plains.

Waldo then asked his Uncle Frank if knew where Laramie got its name. Frank said he heard it was the name of a French-Canadian who was a beaver trapper in Wyoming, long before the Indians were put on reservations.

Jacques La Ramie was a free trapper around the North Platte River in 1820, and was killed by Indians.

Around 8:00 that evening, the three rode through the bustling city of Laramie toward the stockyards south of town. At a cafe near the Stockyard Hotel, they ate steaks and mashed potatoes for dinner.

Frank and Waldo turned in after dinner, but Chic went looking for a bar, so he could get a drink of whiskey and a game of cards.

Though the hotel bed was more comfortable than sleeping on the bare ground, Waldo's rest that night was disturbed because of the noise of horses and wagon traffic, piano music from a saloon down the street, and an occasional gun shot ringing out in the evening air. Waldo wished he could have closed the window, but it was too hot in the hotel and there was a strong stale smell of old cigar smoke lingering in the room.

Friday nights were wild times in Laramie. The city had had a college since 1887, in addition to old Fort Sanders, a brick factory, a brewery, and many other enterprises. It had a large transient population of gamblers, hunters, cowboys, workers, peddlers and straggling settler families. There was an occasional brawl and shooting. The city had been known as having a strong militant vigilante committee that advocated many of the lawless types.

On Saturday morning, Uncle Frank was shaving when Waldo woke from his restless sleep to the sound of wagon wheels and horses' hooves clattering outside.

"How'd you sleep?" Frank asked Waldo.

"I was comfortable, but I kept waking up," Waldo said. "Too much noise."

"Yeah, same here," Uncle Frank admitted.

They met Chic in the restaurant, where they downed steak, eggs, bread and lots of coffee. Chic had a hangover and looked sick. He said he was half-shot, had lost five dollars at cards, and felt stupid about it. The horse sales would start at 1 p.m., and Frank told Chic to go get some sleep until 11 a.m., while he and Waldo walked around town. Chic could meet them at the sale to look over the stock.

"Waldo, here's a nickel," Chic said, "Get me a couple of George Washington Tobacco cut plug pouches, and you can keep the change."

"Thanks!" Waldo replied. Tobacco was a penny a pouch and that left Waldo with three pennies for himself. Maybe he'd get himself a new red bandanna to keep the dust out of his mouth and nose when he rode drag.

Waldo and Frank walked north up Custer Street to Fourth Street and wandered around the shops, looking in the windows. Most of the buildings were two or three stories tall, made of wood or brick,

and had false fronts, squared at the tops. There were boardwalks and hitching rails, with horses tied to them. They came to a mercantile and went in. Waldo got the two pouches of tobacco for Chic, bought a pouch of Laredo Cut Plug for D.J., and picked up a red bandanna with a white flower petal design on the edge for two cents. Frank got his wife some toilet water and a white lacy handkerchief.

They walked past the bank and the barber shop. Frank saw a boot shop across the street called "The Boot Jack." He wanted to see if he could have the loose heel on his right boot fixed.

The shop was full of boots and shoes with tags on them, waiting for their owners to pay for their repairs. This shop also had a cobbler who made boots. As Uncle Frank sat back on a bench reading the paper with one boot on and the other off, Waldo watched the man fix the heel.

When he had finished the repair job, he told Frank that he had a pair of cowboy boots that might fit Waldo, for two dollars, if he was interested. He'd seen Waldo's beat-up shoes when he came into the shop. Waldo's eyes opened wide when he heard what the cobbler said.

"Let's see if they fit," Uncle Frank said. Waldo sat down and pulled off his old shoes as the man brought out a pair of new high-top boots, made of brown leather with short mule ear pulls and high square heels. Waldo pulled them on, stood up, and walked around. There was a bit of room in the toe area but they were a good tight fit everywhere else.

"How they feel?," Uncle Frank asked.

"Great!" Waldo answered.

Frank scratched his head. "I don't know, two dollars is a lot of money," he said.

"A dollar and seventy five is as cheap as I can go," the cobbler replied.

Waldo held his breath and looked at Frank. "I'll give you a dollar and a half and that's it."

"Sold!" agreed the bootmaker, knowing he'd still made money on the deal. Frank paid the man and they walked out, Waldo wearing a great big smile.

"Thanks, Uncle Frank, thanks!," Waldo grinned.

"Happy early birthday," Frank said. Waldo's birthday wasn't for another month. As they walked off, Waldo stopped and re-set his pant legs in the new boots, then caught up to Frank.

At about 11 a.m., they headed for the stockyards and the horse sale to see what was to be bought and sold. Not only the Army, but also others had horses and stock for sale. In fact, there were almost two hundred horses for sale, just as the newspaper ad had promised.

There was a swarm of people on hand for the sale, but Frank and Waldo found Chic in the crowd and Waldo gave him the two pouches of George Washington.

"Hey! New boots and a neck rag, Waldo," Chic noticed.

"Yeah, Unc got me the boots and I bought the bandana with some of the change left from the nickel you gave me."

"Well," Frank said, changing the subject, "see any horses that might be worthwhile?"

Chic said he had and proceeded to point them out to Frank. There were all sorts of horses, even "fantails" or "broomtails," mares with colts and fillies, all barefooted (unshod), and a nice Appaloosa with a good-looking blanket pattern on its rump and blue Sioux eyes, or moon eyes, as some called them.

"Looks like they got a fair share of jug and knot heads here too," Frank declared.

"Yeah, and there's a good-looking black stallion that's a croppy," Chic said. Croppy is an outlaw horse with its ears cropped for identification. "He looks like a Wassup to me." Wassup is a term for a man-killer horse.

By 6 p.m., Frank Korn had purchased eight horses to add to the ranch stock, or cavvy. That night, the threesome stayed at the hotel, after another good meal in the cafe. This time Chic didn't bother to go to the saloon as he was down to his last dollar, which he chose to hang onto for a while.

The next morning, Waldo pulled on his new boots with pride. By 6 a.m., the three rode west out of Laramie, heading back to the K Bar Ranch with the eight new horses in tow.

It took them three and a half days to get back because they ran into some "Oklahoma rain"—a sand and dust storm—and had to stay hunkered down until it blew over.

Waldo was glad to have his new bandana to cover his nose and mouth. And when the storm was over, they still had the eight horses with them. This was lucky because they couldn't see more than two or three feet in front of them during the storm. Sometimes stock will move for miles with the wind to their backs.

The ranch sure looked good to Waldo, who was happy to have his own bed to sleep in that night. By then, his boots had formed to his feet and they felt great for riding.

Chapter 5

THINGS ON the ranch were somewhat busy for the next few days. D.J. and Chic branded the new horses with the K Bar brand and took turns riding them to see how they handled.

Of the eight horses, four were bays, brown with black manes and tails. One was a gelding with a white star on its forehead, two of the bay mares had white socks, and the fourth bay was a gelding with a blazed face. The bays were former Army horses and so had the U.S. brand on their left hips. Two of the other horses were geldings, sorrels—red horses with red tails and manes—also with the U.S. brands, and the last two included a white mare and a palomino mare—a cream-colored horse with a white tail and mane.

Because of the continuous growth of the hoof, horses need to be shod every six to ten weeks. An active horse's hooves will grow faster than those of inactive ones. Uncle Frank's new horses were all overdue to have their hooves trimmed and re-shod.

It was going to be D.J.'s job to make shoes and to shoe the horses. Waldo was told to help and learn. The horses were kept in the corral next to the barn, where it later was discovered that there were a couple of cribbers and a stump sucker in the bunch.

Of the eight horses, one was cold-jawed and one of the Army bays was dead-mouthed. A cold-jawed horse is one with a hard

GOOD LUCK

mouth, while one whose mouth had become insensitive to the bit is known as dead-mouthed. The palomino was a cloud watcher. She traveled with her head too high to watch the cattle work. And two of the Army bays seemed to be rope shy. Other than these few bad habits, however, they would, in time, become good ranch stock with the proper training and care.

One morning after breakfast, D.J. and Waldo headed to the barn to tack iron on the new horses. Just outside the barn was an added-on shed roof that covered the Acme portable forge with its hand-cranked fan blower, the eagle anvil and the tongs, hammers, shoeing iron, coal, nails and a water barrel.

Waldo got the coal burning in the forge, while D.J. brought one of the horses in to be shod. Waldo would turn the crank on the blower to get the coal to burn.

D.J. tied the halter rope to the hitching post and started first by lifting a foreleg of the horse up between his knees, which he clamped firmly together, leaving both hands free to clean the hoof with a pick and brush.

"Watch what I'm doin' and ya git to handle the next one," D.J. told Waldo. "When taking off the shoe, don't wrench it violently, but draw it off easy and slow. First, lift the clinched nail tips with the clinch cutter, then lift the entire shoe slightly with the broad-billed pinchers. Then use the pinchers to finish the job by moving them only in the direction of the branches of the horseshoe," D.J. explained.

"Also, don't twist the hoof," he continued. "Keep it supported with the left hand or with your leg just above the knee. Twisting the hoof can strain the ligaments and ya end up with a lame horse. Ya got to remember that trimming is most important. Have to shorten the hoof that keeps a growin' too long under the shoe."

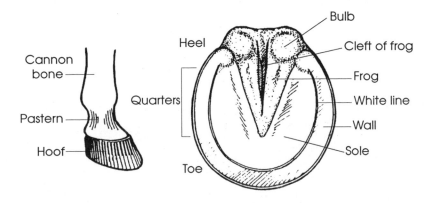

D.J. had placed the rasping file, cutting nippers and the hoof knife within his reach, but away from the horse he was working. To hasten the work, D.J. used the nippers on the hard black hoofs. He examined each hoof and limb, removing the loose and detached portions of the wall, and scraped off the flakes of dead horn from the sole. Then he ran the rasp around the wall and broke it off at the proper depth.

"Now in dressin' the frog, always leave it so that it will project beyond the bearing surface, about the thickness of the shoe," D.J. told Waldo. "Never trim the frog at all."

Now it was time to start making horseshoes.

"Waldo, to make a shoe the right size, ya find the length of the hoof from the angles of the heel to the toe and width, and added together ya git the length of bar needed," D.J. explained.

"Ya heat the bar to a white heat just beyond the middle. Turn the blower handle to git the coals hotter."

When the iron bar was heated to the correct temperature, D.J. put the bar on the flat of the anvil and ran over it lightly with the hammer to flatten it. He heated it again, set it back on the anvil and started the right bend of the branch, after which he began to put the fuller, or groove, in the right branch of the shoe. Then he stamped four holes for the nails and punched them through with the pritcher, and finally hammered the bearing sides perfectly smooth and horizontal. D.J. then repeated the process on the left branch of the shoe until he had a complete shoe made. Next, he sized the shoe, shaped it to the horse's hoof and, on the anvil, hammered it to the right fit.

Before D.J. started to put that shoe on the horse, he put a slight curve in the nail he was going to use to fasten the shoe down.

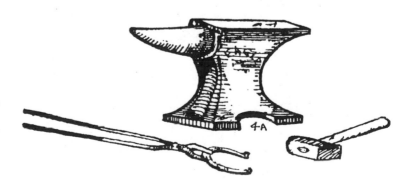

He then picked up the shoeing hammer and began nailing the shoe, bending down the nail points toward the shoe.

"Hammer them down and, usin' the pinchers, bend them more," D.J. said. "Nip off the points near the hoof and rasp off the horn that has been broken out."

Using a cinch block under the nail heads, D.J. then clinched them still closer to the walls of the hoof with the edge of the hammer, the nail driven down flush with the wall.

By the time they had four of the horses shod, it was almost meal time and D.J. had Waldo trying his hand at making a horseshoe. With some difficulty and D.J.'s helping hand, Waldo got his first horseshoe made.

"You're gettin' the hang of it, Waldo," D.J. told him. "I'll make a hoof-shaper and iron tacker out of you yet."

Just then, the dinner triangle rang out and they headed for a wash up and noon chuck.

After the meal, they went back to pulling off old shoes, trimming hooves, and building horseshoes. They finished shoeing the eight new horses, as well as two of the other ranch horses. Waldo learned that a white hoof was made of softer horn than a black hoof and easier to trim. Hooves are made of the same material as cow horns.

That night was clear as crystal with a light wind. The cowboys were all sitting out on the top rail of the corral, rolling coffin nails and telling Waldo stories. Charlie recalled one time when he was cowboying in Oklahoma on the Slash Lazy S when his boss had gotten himself an arbuckle for a jingler just before the big cow drive to Kansas.

"Well, one mornin'," Charlie remembered, "this here arbuckle was headin' in the corral to get his mount and, just as he was about to

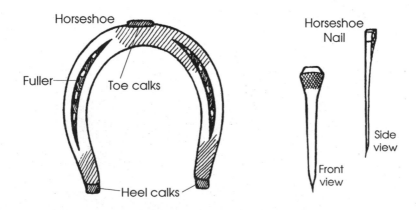

Horseshoe
Fuller
Toe calks
Heel calks

Horseshoe Nail
Front view
Side view

throw his loop over his mount, this here nice kitty (skunk), which was a rootin' around the corral, got into a frenzy and let loose with its stink. Ya could smell it clear to the stars. Well, I'll tell ya, all the horses got a whiff of that smell and they bolted, broke out of the corral and were hell-bent broncos. It took two days to catch them and, when we did, they were lathered to the teeth. We got them settled down, but just as we got back to the ranch and are passin' by the outhouse, out walks that jingler, hoisting up his suspenders and still smelling like a skunk. Those horses smelled him, and all but one broke loose from us and headed for open range again."

D.J., Chic and Waldo roared with laughter.

"The boss was so mad that I thought he was going to have that arbuckle strung up and riddled with lead," Charlie adding, drawing more chortles.

"Yeah, the boss made him wash himself and his clothes every day till the smell was gone. And once the jingler was clean of the skunky smell, he up and quits the Slash Lazy S and says he's going to join the Army." Waldo laughed along with D.J,. and Chic coughed out his cigarette with the chuckles.

D.J. then started a story of his own "We had a biskit shooter that, once in a while, would make what the old trappers called bear sign, which was some dough fried up in fat, and then he'd sugar them up—this was a real treat to all the waddies," he began. "But this one waddie had such a sweet tooth—and also seemed to know when the cook was going to make them—that he'd always find some way of yamping a half dozen for himself without someone seeing him do it. Next time Cookie decided to make bear sign, he took some chili powder and mixed it in a bunch of dough, sugared the top and set the plate out in plain sight and turned his

back on them. When he turned around again, half the signs were missin'. All of a sudden, there was this waddie whoopin' and hollerin' and coughin'. Then he sticks his head under the water spigot and darn near drank the whole barrel!"

Everyone snickered again, as D.J. finished: "That sure cured his sweet tooth."

"It wouldn't have if he'd been a Mexican," Chic added. "They like their grub hotter than a cookstove."

Next, it was Chic's turn. He started a story about the time he was hazin' in an area of mesquite and cactus-infested desert, all full of fierce thorns.

"What the thorns can't do to you and your pony, the sun sure can," Chic began. "Anyhow, I'd come across this steer with eight-foot horns on him and set my horse to cut him in with the others. Then I noticed he was droolin' like he'd just drunk up the Rio Grande River. He turned and hooked my pony with one horn and flipped us both into some cactus. The horse was OK. Broke the saddle cinch, though, and it took me the rest of the day to get all the thorns out of my hide—with the help of another cowboy. The steer had gotten into some locoweed and was out there in the bush walking in a circle. Boss had him shot."

This story didn't bring out any laughs, but Chic went on. "I tell you this was my most unlucky week because three days later I started scratchin' all over myself. Well, I'd picked up a whole family of Seam Squirrels (lice) and couldn't wait to get back to the rancho and get myself dipped to kill the little critters." Now it was funny.

Waldo didn't have any stories to tell but he knew that if he kept his mouth closed and his eyes and ears open, he would learn from the experiences of others and, one day, he would have tales of his own to share.

Chapter 6

IT WAS a sunny, hot Saturday with not even a breeze to keep the bugs from biting. In July, the mosquito population exploded. Each year, Waldo thought that they were worse than the year before.

At 7 a.m., Waldo was doing his chores. He had just picked up an armload of firewood for the stove, when he looked up to the west. In the distance, he could see someone heading toward him on horseback. He took the wood into the kitchen and set it in the woodbox.

"There's a rider headin' in, but can't make him out," Waldo announced. "Might be a hand from the Double X. He's on a dark horse."

Mr. Korn headed for a west window while setting his hand on the holstered gun hanging on his right hip. Looking out the window, he studied the advancing rider.

"That's no horse, Waldo; it's a mule," Frank said. "Still can't tell who's on it."

Ten minutes later, the mule rider, a black man, was at the front of the ranch house with Cheyenne barking up a storm.

"I'm a nu handa wit da Doub X an Mister Monte told me ta ride here an ask if yous seen any a da X cows mixed wit yourn," the rider said.

"I'm Frank Korn and this here's Waldo." Waldo nodded to the rider and he nodded back.

"Now that the dog is settled down, you can step off that jack and come in for a cup of coffee," Frank said. "It's still hot."

"Ma name's Willie an I been workin' fur Mister Monte fur a bit now," the man said, holding his hat in his hands.

"Well, Willie, there hasn't been any of the Double X stock on this side of the Medicine Bow, except for a couple of your horses that mixed in with our string a couple days ago. You can cut them out and back if you need them," Frank told him.

"Thanks fur da coffee, Mister. I better get da hosses and head back, but da truth of da madder is dat dares about fifteen hosses out of our herd dat no one's seen in a bit."

"You tell Monte I'll send word to him if any of my hands spot his stock," Frank said.

"Mister Monte is thinkin' dars sometin' goin' on," Willie said, "but wanted to make sure dat dey weren't on this side of da river."

"Well," Frank said, "we haven't seen hide nor hair of the cows you're asking about. If we do, we'll round them up for you."

Waldo had Buck saddled and was ready as Willie came out of the house with Frank.

"Waldo will help you jingle the horses out."

They both rode south along the river in silence.

Finally, Waldo spoke. "Chances are that the horses are just over the rise," he said. "D.J. said he'd seen them there yesterday, eating buffalo grass."

Willie nodded. He wasn't too tall, but had a stocky build. He was as dark as his mule, and wore overalls, a plaid shirt, a well-worn straw hat and scuffed-up work shoes that looked big and heavy.

"How long you been riding that mule?" Waldo asked.

"Walters an me's been togedder fur bout goin' on twenty years now, an reckon we'd got an odder five to ten years. He's old but still woks hard."

When they had reached an area called Tableland, just north of the confluence of the East Medicine Bow River and the main river, they spotted the horses, swishing their tails and shaking their manes in an effort to keep the bugs off.

"I know for sure the black and the appie horse are Double X stock," Waldo told Willie as he slapped at the bugs behind his ears. Willie seemed oblivious to the bugs' bites as they sucked out his blood.

As they got closer to the horses, Willie declared: "Dat bay mare hoss wit da saddle sore spots at da whithers, we been lookin' fur also. Darn, she looks poor; she's puttin' on weight bad!"

Willie and Waldo cut the three horses out of the herd. Willie headed for the Double X mounts across the river and Waldo cut the K Bar horses off from following.

They rode west along Pass Creek for a while and then turned north toward Jack Hill and the Double X Ranch headquarters, three miles ahead. When they got to the ranch, the hands were just sitting down to noon chuck and Waldo joined in the meal before heading back to the K Bar.

There was talk about the other missing horses, and one of the hands said he thought that there were some heifers missing around the lower end of the ranch too. It was suggested that maybe the horses had run off with a bunch of broomtails, though it wasn't likely because the head stallion of the wild bunch wouldn't allow any of the missing geldings to run with his herd of mares, colts, and fillies.

After the meal, one of the hands asked Waldo if he could read, and Waldo told them yes, he could. Many cowboys lacked education and couldn't read or write. Waldo was lucky that he had had schooling and Auntie made sure he kept up his reading and writing skills.

"Good," said the Double X hand, "I've got a book for you to read. I've read it over a dozen times and I think it's time I passed it on to another to read for a bit."

"Really?," Waldo exclaimed.

"It's called *The Last of The Mohicans*, by James Fenimore Cooper. He's a real good writer and I think you'll enjoy it."

"Thanks a lot," Waldo said. "I'll get it back to you as soon as I read it."

Waldo wrapped the tattered book in an old newspaper and put it in his saddle bag. He refilled his canteen, said his good-byes, saddled up, turned Buck toward the K Bar, and set off at a trot.

The afternoon was hotter than the morning. Waldo had Buck walking now. No real hurry to get back to the ranch, Waldo thought. He pulled off his hat and wiped his forehead and the inside of his hat band. Suddenly, Buck raised her head and pricked her ears forward.

Waldo set his hat back on and looked to see what had won Buck's attention. Up ahead, a stream of dirt was being thrown out of the ground.

"Buck, that's nothing to worry about," Waldo assured. "It's just a badger late at digging his noon chuck. Probably a ground squirrel or gopher. We'll just stay clear of him. Don't want him getting mad at us and charging, do we, Buck?"

Just then, the badger's head popped out of the hole and he growled some before going back to his digging.

Then, as they crossed a hardpan area—stone-covered ground—Waldo realized that Buck had a loose rear shoe. It was making a clicking noise, and he'd have to fix it when he got back to the ranch. Waldo reined Buck to a stop and got off to check the shoe, but there wasn't much he could do about it. If it got thrown, he'd just have to build a new one.

As Waldo was stepping back into the stirrup, he thought he heard voices coming from near the river ahead of him. Before starting out, he sat on Buck and listened. Buck's ears were up and they both searched for the sound of voices, but nothing was to be heard, except the distant caw of a raven flying over the river. Then the raven perched on the upper-most branch of a half-dead cottonwood. That tree may have been hit by lightening, Waldo thought.

The raven cawed again and flew off. That's when Waldo noticed a trace of light blue smoke coming from the willows. Odd, Waldo thought, wondering who would be camped there. Must have made a fire to keep the bugs away, but there wasn't a lot of smoke, so no one was burning any green sage or willow to create a heavy smoke. Bad place to camp, Waldo thought. The mosquitoes must be thick as thieves.

Waldo rode forward at a slow walk. When he reached the willows, he dismounted and tied Buck to a bunch of willow. Then he heard someone speak.

"Roy, you and Hank get goin' now so you'll cover ground 'fore dark. We'll take off at first light with the cows and we'll have them re-branded by tomorrow."

Waldo didn't recognize the voice. He couldn't see much from

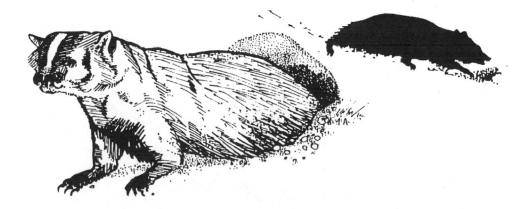

where he was, so he made his way along the cow trail in the willows and thistle to where he could see what was going on. There, he caught sight of some cowboys with about a dozen range horses. Waldo backtracked as quietly as he could. Fortunately, there was a bit of commotion with the two cowboys getting ready to move out the horses and Waldo made it back to where Buck was without being discovered. He untied his horse and walked her down the west side of the river toward Dutch Highlands. Once he was out of ear-shot, he crossed the river and rode hard for the K Bar Ranch to warn Uncle Frank.

About two miles from the ranch, Waldo came upon Chic and D.J. When he told them what he had seen, D.J. told Chic to ride to the Double X and that he and Waldo were to get Frank and they'd all meet at Dutch Highland by the Big Indian Picture Rock before heading after the thieves.

When Waldo and D.J. got to the ranch, Waldo told Uncle Frank about the conversation he'd heard and how he had watched one of the cinch-ring artists re-branding a Double X heifer. Frank got the rifles, carbines and ammunition. Then they rode off, leaving Charlie and Mrs. Korn to watch over the place.

The three got to Dutch Highlands at about 5 p.m. At Picture Rock, they waited for Chic and the Double X boss and hands.

"Should I go see what the rustlers are up to?" D.J. asked Frank.

"No, the gang from the Double X will be here in a bit. Then we'll all ride in and ambush the rattlesnakes."

Waldo got off Buck to look at the loose shoe, which was still holding. As he set Buck's hoof down to the ground, he saw something in the dirt. He reached down and picked up a brown piece of stone, an arrowhead.

"Look!," Waldo said excitedly to Frank and D J., holding the point up between his thumb and trigger finger.

"That's good luck for you, Waldo," Frank said. "It don't even have a nick in it."

"What's it made of?," Waldo asked.

"Looks like agate to me—or maybe chert," D.J. said. On closer examination, though, D.J. made a positive identification. "Aah, it's agate," he explained. "And see these here sharp little spikes up and down the two edges? That's so it'll cut through the bone."

Chic and the Double X men arrived by 6:30 p.m. They all rested for a while, and formed a plan. When they got close to the rustlers, they would go on foot and surround them, catching them by surprise, which might reduce the likelihood of shooting.

They all rode their horses at a walk toward the thieves' camp to the south. About a mile from the camp, the K Bar hands crossed the river again, while the six men from the Double X stayed on the west side.

The plan was that the Double X men would jump the branding artists while the K Bar hands kept them from making a run for it across the river.

"If there's shooting when we git there, I want you to find cover and stay hunkered down," Frank told Waldo. "I don't want you catchin' any lead."

"Maybe Monte will just spill his loop over the two rustlers and there won't be any shootin'," Waldo said.

"Don't bet on it," Frank responded.

As they got closer, everyone dismounted. Waldo was told to hold the horses for Frank, D.J. and Chic, while they snuck up to the camp. The Double X bunch approached from the other side of the river.

Waldo waited, holding the reins of the three horses and hoping they would not whinny to the rustlers' horses or the Double X horses.

Then he heard George, owner of the Double X, yell out, "You men are surrounded! Get your hands reachin' for the sky or we'll shoot!"

But one of the rustlers grabbed for his six gun and the other ran for his horse. The gunfire lasted only two seconds, and the two men lay dead.

"Waldo, bring the horses!," Frank hollered out.

When Waldo got there, he saw what the rustlers had been up to. In the willows, they had built a makeshift corral out of brush. Inside the corral were a number of cows with new brands, triple diamonds.

The Double X brands had been altered into triple diamonds.

At the camp fire was a cinch-ring running iron that they picked up with a couple of green cut willow sticks when it was hot enough for branding.

Two of the Double X men were to stay behind and take care of the corpses, and the evidence of rustling, while the rest rode on, following the tracks of the stolen horses.

By 10 p.m., it was dark, but there was a full moon and Willie was able to keep sight of the horse tracks. At midnight, they made a dry camp and slept until 4:30 a.m. Everyone was saddled and back on the trail by 5:00. No supper and no breakfast left Waldo's stomach growling with hunger. No one had bothered to bring food with them, and there wasn't time to cook it if they had.

They rode hard but not at a gallop, as they didn't want to overheat the horses, plus it looked like they were getting close to the stolen horses and thieves.

When they got to Elk Hollow Creek, the tracks followed the water, heading toward the Platte River.

"They must be headin' for the Colorado border," George said.

Just before they reached the Platte, they rested the horses and sent two riders ahead to scout. Shortly, the riders came back, announcing that the thieves were camped ahead a couple of miles.

"Doesn't look like they're in any hurry, and they got our horses," one of the scouts said.

A plan was made to circle around the two and catch them by surprise before they could get their guns. This turned out to be easy, as the two horse thieves had not bothered posting guard and were casually drinking coffee and smoking their last cigarettes.

"No one put up a fight," George said. "This time, we weren't hampered by the hoss thieves goin' for their guns."

Justice was fast in those days. There wasn't a lot of law, lawyers, or judges, so vigilantes acted as all three—as well as executioners. The trial for the two men lasted a minute or two, and they were found guilty. Nooses were made from two reatas, and a cottonwood tree served as gallows for the thieves.

Waldo saw his first hanging and reckoned that walking on the wrong side of the law meant a short life.

It took the rest of the day to wrangle the horses back after burying the two thieves.

Back at the ranch, the tired men ate dinner without much chatter. No one felt very good about the shooting and hangings, but it had to be done or others too lazy to work would turn to stealing from those who did toil.

Waldo turned in as soon as he had eaten. In the morning, he would replace Buck's thrown shoe. He lay in his bunk with his new book, *The Last Of The Mohicans*, and he turned his lantern up bright. Tomorrow, he would ask Auntie Korn to sew the arrowhead on his hat for him.

He began reading: "It was a feature peculiar to the colonial wars of North America, that the toils and dangers of the wilderness were to be encountered before the adverse hosts could meet." Waldo read on until he could keep his eyes open no longer.

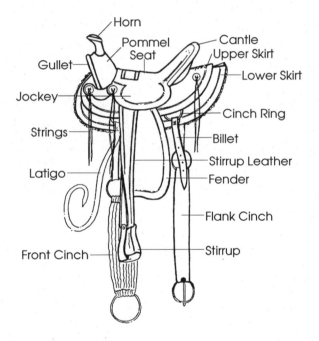

Horn
Pommel
Seat
Cantle
Upper Skirt
Gullet
Lower Skirt
Jockey
Cinch Ring
Strings
Billet
Stirrup Leather
Latigo
Fender
Flank Cinch
Front Cinch
Stirrup

WALDO AWOKE to Uncle Frank's calling: "Rise and shine, you're burning daylight, Waldo." He jumped from his bunk where he had been dreaming about Cheyenne hunting prairie dogs the size of jackrabbits.

That morning after chores, Waldo made Buck a new shoe to replace the one he'd lost. Charlie already had left for town to get supplies and would be back in the late afternoon. Waldo was to cruise up Wagonhound Creek and check the stock, and look up in the forest for a stand of dead lodgepole pine for he and Charlie to down for firewood.

After saddling Buck, Waldo went into the ranch-house kitchen and got some biscuits and jerky to take with him. He didn't want to be without food as he was the two days before.

It was another hot day, with a warm breeze and an occasional gust of wind that would create sometimes-large dust devils. Some were only a foot or two high, while others grew as large as fifteen feet tall and lasted a minute or so. They carried sand, grass, sticks and alkali dust into the air; they were small tornadoes.

On a large bench across from Wagonhound Creek—just a trickle of water at this time of the year—were burrows of a large

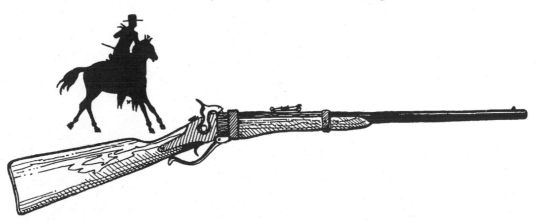

prairie-dog community. The animals would rise on their haunches, hold their forepaws together across their chests, rolling small balls of grass between them. They'd bark shrilly and dive down the closest burrow or scamper to another hole, as Cheyenne ran full speed after them. Cheyenne was always running after something, usually a jackrabbit breaking from cover and speeding around sage and greasewood in leaps of six to ten feet or more.

Waldo's thoughts were on the dream he had had that morning—and the fact that in a week he would be another year older. His birthday was on July 16. He wondered if Auntie Korn would make him a birthday cake like she always had in the past. One thing was for sure: He was glad to have his new boots to ride in, long before his birthday.

He rode up into the forest and found a couple of large stands of beetle-killed lodgepole pine that would make good firewood and that was easy to get to with the wagon and team. He had cruised a large area and had seen no trouble with the stock.

By now, Cheyenne was starting to run out of steam and no longer chased ahead, but followed at Buck's heels as they headed back to the ranch. In the distance, Waldo could see a golden eagle soaring on the wind, with its wings spread out to nearly eight feet. It was hunting.

When Waldo got back to the ranch in the late afternoon, Charlie was already back from Elk Mountain with supplies and the news of the weeks past. Two of the newspapers, only a month old, told of the June 2 Wilcox train robbery, in which the bandits got away with an estimated $60,000. Wilcox was a railroad town about thirty miles northeast of the K Bar, as the crow flies, and eight or so miles north of the town of Rock River.

The front page of the Laramie paper headlined the train robbery. It told of two men who flagged a Union Pacific Railroad train and, with revolvers drawn, ordered the engineer to cut the engine, express, and baggage cars loose and to pull across the bridge beyond Wilcox and stop. They dynamited the bridge to prevent the arrival of the second train, which was due in ten minutes. They forced the engineer to run the train two miles west, then looted the express cars and escaped with $60,000 in unsigned bank notes. More than one hundred pounds of dynamite were found near the scene of the robbery the following day. The robbers rode northward and escaped to Montana, it was thought. The paper credited the planning of the robbery to Butch Cassidy and Flat Nose George Currie, but no one knew who really pulled it off.

Waldo had never been to Wilcox, once a stage station for the Overland Stage. He had, however, been to Rock River, which was a bit larger than the town of Elk Mountain. False-front stores, scattered houses and a railroad livestock point made up Rock River. It was a busy place, with lots of freighters, known as bullwhackers, and mule skinners who drove the freight outfits.

Early one morning at the end of the week, Waldo and Charlie put the sideboards on the wagon and loaded the axes and the two-man bucksaw, bedrolls, food and water and headed up to where Waldo had found the stand of dead trees.

They worked until dark cutting down the trees, sawing them into manageable lengths, and loading up the wagon with more than a cord of wood. They used the team of horses to move the long-fallen trees closer to the wagon, and then cut them there. Then they set up camp for the night.

After dark, they listened to the nighthawks woring, or making vibrant buzzes while diving to catch insects at high speeds. They could see them flying about on long pointed wings, with white bars and long, notched tails. The birds would cry out occasionally, "spee-ik" to one another. In the distance, a coyote would cry out and another, a half mile away, would yelp back in answer.

The following morning, they headed back to the ranch and, that afternoon, they again bucked up firewood to stove lengths, and split and stacked the new wood next to the old pile.

"Tomorrow I'll have to re-oil the harness and lines; they're drying out some," Charlie told Waldo.

"I'll help you if Unc doesn't have something already for me to do," Waldo answered.

Early Sunday evening, Chic called out to D.J.: "There's a rider comin' in!"

"I'll tell the boss," D.J. yelled back, as he rode his horse from the corrals to the ranch house, just two hundred yards away. He reached the hitching post as Waldo was coming out. "Waldo, tell Frank dars someone ridin' this way. He don't look local to me."

When Frank came out with Waldo at his heels, the stranger's fast-walking dapple gray horse with four black sox, black mane and tail was at the corrals. He slowed his horse some as he rode toward D.J., who was still sitting on his horse.

"Good evening," the stranger drawled.

"Howdy," everyone greeted back as they watched him advance.

Charlie and Chic were watching from the bunkhouse.

"My name's Walter P. Scaggs, out of Nevada," the man said.

Walter P. Scaggs was a tall man and sat straight in the saddle. He wore a long duster coat that looked like a fish but was made of a cotton cloth. His hat was black, but very dusty, to the point you could not really tell it was black.

Waldo stared at the rider's Spanish silver bit and spurs. The rowels on the spurs were large, and the bit had rein chains. The bridle was made of braided horse hair—the reins too, but with buttons and tuffs.

The horse had an unreadable Mexican style brand on its right front shoulder.

The stranger's saddle was a Mexican charro style, and there were tapaderos on the stirrups. His reata was tied at the back of the saddle. Over the pommel and across Walter P. Scaggs' lap lay a heavy rifle, which Waldo later learned was a Sharps single shot breach loading .45-70 caliber rifle. It was accurate for a fairly long range, had a peep sight for what was known as a rainbow trajectory at a longer distance, and had good stopping power. Sharps were used by the U.S. Cavalry mostly—and the Indians, when they could get a hold of one.

Under his duster, Scaggs carried two holstered Colt revolvers with stained white bone grips.

"I'd appreciate any hospitality you might extend me," Scaggs said. "I'm willin' to pay for a meal and oats for my horse."

"I'm sure the Mrs. can rustle up somethin', and you're welcome to sleep in the bunkhouse or barn if you want," Frank told him.

"Thank you," Scaggs said, "I'd like to take care of my horse first."

"Waldo, show the man where the grain bin is in the barn. Then, when you're ready, come on back and have a bite to eat," Frank said.

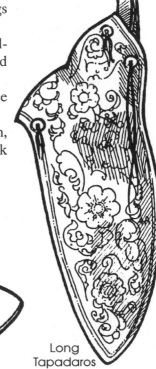

Long
Tapadaros

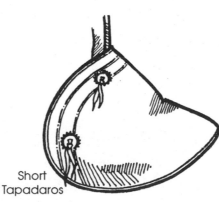

Short
Tapadaros

Mrs. Korn had put the coffee pot on, was frying up some meat and beans for the stranger and had set up a cup and plate for him at the table by the time he and Waldo returned to the house. Frank was sitting at the table with a cup of coffee.

"I appreciate your kindness, ma'am," Scaggs said as he entered the house and pulled his hat from his head. "I reckon you've guessed that I'm a regulator."

"Yeah," Frank answered. "I figured you to be a bounty hunter."

Scaggs didn't look up from the meal. "What brings me this far is, I got a wire about the Wilcox train holdup from the U.P. Railroad detectives. We're working together on trying to catch the Wild Bunch."

The Wild Bunch was also known as the Powder Springs Gang because they were believed to have gone there—near Baggs, Wyoming—to celebrate holdups in surrounding states, including a $35,000 haul in Winnemucca, Nevada. The gang took over Baggs and threw money and bullets around. The outlaws did, however, pay generously for any of the property they destroyed so the town did profit from them.

Frank and Scaggs talked about the train robbery. Waldo listened to the stranger's story of hunting the Wild Bunch in Nevada, Utah, Idaho and Wyoming. There was talk about the outlaw hideout called the Hole in the Wall, which was somewhere in central Wyoming near the headwaters of the Powder River.

Scaggs told Frank that if they ever found where the Hole in the Wall was located, he reckoned the law would be all over the gang like blowflies on a dead heifer.

Walter P. Scaggs was a lean-faced man with icy blue-green eyes. He sported a long graying handlebar moustache and, when he moved his legs under the kitchen table, the rowels of his silver spurs would sing out in a clear tone. Scaggs was a serious man; you could tell he meant business.

The next morning, Walter P. Scaggs saddled his horse, thanked the Korns, paid for the food, and rode northeast toward the town of Wilcox and the trail of the robbers. Waldo thought to himself that the man had a lot of riding ahead of him.

Waldo had almost forgotten about his birthday when July 16 rolled around. Of course, everyone made believe they had forgotten about it too but, at noon, the triangle rang extra loud and everyone was there on time. Waldo got a cake and presents. D.J. gave Waldo a set of cuffs he'd made for him out of good saddle leather. And Charlie produced a rawhide quirt he'd braided some time ago. Monte had braided a horse-hair stampede string for Waldo's hat, which had blown off his head more than once in the past. Waldo was now 15 years old, almost a man. Auntie and Uncle had given Waldo a silver dollar, as well as the boots. Waldo now felt rich and, that evening, he looked through the beat-up Sears Roebuck catalog at the rifles. In particular, he had his eyes on a Winchester .25-20 carbine, model 1892, with a 20-inch barrel, saddle ring, and a $10.95 price tag, shipping extra. He'd have to find a way to make $10 more, and that would take a long time. But Waldo knew that anything worth having is worth working and waiting for.

Chapter 8

THE WEEKS that followed Waldo's birthday were busy. He and Charlie spent most of the time out in the forest cutting firewood. By now, they had cut, split and stacked eight cords of mostly lodge-pole pine, in addition to a small amount of spruce. No one liked using spruce because it would crack in the fire and throw sparks and it also was often full of knots and very difficult to split. What they needed now was one cord of aspen for Auntie Korn's cookstove. They would cut that over near the beaver ponds and line shack number two.

Today was Sunday and pretty much a dink-around-the-ranch day. Charlie had left the work wagon parked in the Medicine Bow River overnight, up to the hubs in water, and would move it once a day so that the wheels would soak. The wheels had dried out, the spokes were loose in the hubs, and the wood and metal iron rim, known as a tire, would rattle a little. By leaving the wheels in the water, the wood would soak up moisture and swell, making everything tight again for a while.

Outside the bunkhouse, the magpies were clammering about something. Cheyenne joined in by barking up a storm. Chic was rolling up a coffin nail when he decided to step out to see what the commotion was about. There, in the sandy ground, Chic heard a T-sssss sound! A large rattlesnake was sounding its warning, just before striking out. It sprang out at Cheyenne, but the dog jumped away in time. The snake re-coiled and rattled again. Chic called Cheyenne off and fired his revolver as the snake struck out again, trying to get its poison fangs into the dog. Rattlesnakes are called "gentlemen snakes" because they give warning before they strike. Chic had shot the head off the diamond-back rattler.

Everyone had rushed out to see what was happening. Charlie approached the snake and held it up. It was a good three feet long with six rattles, not counting the button tip.

"Well," Charlie said, looking at Chic, "you shot it, you going to eat it?"

"I don't eat no snakes or lizards," Chic said as he holstered his gun again.

"If you're not eating it, me and Waldo will have it for lunch tomorrow."

"It's all yours—and Waldo can make a hat band out of its hide, Chic said, adding, "Cheyenne's dumber than a stick going after the rattler; good thing he's fast."

Charlie skinned out the snake, and Waldo salted it and tacked it to the barn door to dry. Charlie cut strips of meat off the snake's bony frame, salted and floured them, wrapped them in some calico cloth, and set them in the cool screened pie safe.

"I'll fry it up in a little salt-pork fat, Waldo," Charlie said. "Chic don't know what he's missin'; snakes are good eatin'." Waldo wasn't sure, but he trusted Charlie's judgment and was willing to try something new.

The previous evening, Waldo had retrieved an old lard can

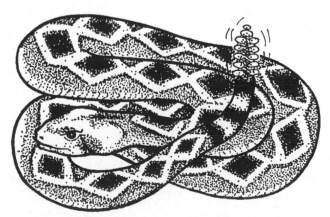

half full of worms out of the garden so that he and Charlie would have fishing bait. Now they walked down the river looking for a good fishing hole. The mud swallows were very active, flying about catching insects and then back to their mud nests hanging off the underside of looming sandstone cliffs. When Charlie and Waldo found a good hole, they each made a fishing pole from long strong branches. They attached string to the thinner end of the sticks, tied hooks to the free ends, and split spent-bullet leads they had retrieved from the spot where everyone practiced shooting at cans and bottles and made weights out of them. Each of them put a weight about 16 inches up from the hook to keep the bait from floating up in the water. They tossed their lines into the water hole and waited until a fish took the bait, then set the hook and pulled the fish out of the water and onto the bank. They fished until they caught enough to feed everyone. The cutthroat trout were a nice size, and the one sucker fish Waldo had on his hook, he released back into the water. After cleaning the fish at the river, they walked back to the ranch with plenty for dinner.

Monday came fast. Waldo and Charlie hitched the team to the wagon and headed for the beaver ponds and aspen groves at daybreak. By mid-morning, they were hard at work, cutting wood about a mile from line shack number two. The area had a couple of large beaver ponds; green aspen had been felled by the beavers for food and construction materials.

All of the beaver-cut stumps had been shaped by their sharp chisel teeth, as if by an axe. Occasionally, Waldo heard a loud splash in one of the ponds, as a beaver hit its large flat tail on the water in warning to other beavers of possible danger.

At this time of year, the pastures around the aspen groves were in full bloom with flowers—purple-pink fireweed, orange-red Indian paintbrush, light pink wild rose, blue lupine and yellow daisies. Fields with all the colors of the rainbow.

When they took a break for noon chuck, Charlie cooked up the rattlesnake meat and then ate it with cold biscuits and hot black coffee. To Waldo's surprise, he really liked the meat—kind of like chicken, he thought.

"Looks like we've got a leak in the side of this old coffee pot," Charlie said.

He pulled his three-bladed cattleman's folding knife from his pocket and cut a stick to plug the hole in the side of the fire-blackened enamel coffee pot. "There, that should do it for a bit!"

Waldo looked up at the blue sky and said to Charlie, "Look at all those mares' tails; we're going to get some rain later."

"Yup, we'll get the wagon loaded and then spend the night in the line shack."

Mares' tails are cloud formations that are very high in the sky. They are long and thin, sweep across the sky like the hair of a horse's tail, and are the forewarning of an approaching storm.

By afternoon, the wind and dark storm clouds had moved in. The wagon was loaded and the team hitched up, so Charlie and Waldo headed for the small log line shack. It had a sod roof, dirt floor and one small side window made from four clear glass bottles with the necks cut off and stacked side by side in a wooden frame. The shack was chinked with mud and grass, and the rusty stovepipe chimney had a large lard can over its top to protect it from rain and snow. It made a good shelter in bad weather.

After unhitching the team, putting it in the makeshift corral, and placing the harnesses under the wagon for protection, Charlie and Waldo hauled their bedrolls into the dusty shack.

Moments later, the rain started pounding hard on the ground. "We just made it in time," Waldo said. They made a fire in the small iron stove and brewed up some coffee. Waldo looked around the place. It was dusty, there were a few spider webs, and the mice had made a nest of shredded old newspaper—and whatever else they could use—in the corner behind the stove. Thunder and lightening lasted a good part of the night, but the rain finally ceased in the early-morning hours.

After breakfast of coffee and cold biscuits, Charlie headed the team back toward the ranch, keeping the wagon on high ground so it wouldn't get bogged in the mud. The wagon cut deep ruts into the rained-soaked earth as it moved slowly forward. When they got to the track that had been used many times in the past, the going was easier. Small groups of antelope does and their kids dotted the landscape. Now and then, you could see bucks running at top speed or just standing on a hilltop keeping watch.

Back at the ranch that evening, there was talk about the annual August shindig in Elk Mountain. It was, as usual, a pot-luck affair. This meant the women would bring cakes and pies, breads, bean dishes, vegetable dishes, canned goods, jams and everything good to eat. The men of Elk would roast a side of beef. There was food for everyone and, as they said in those days, everyone would partake in a good time. People would come from all the surrounding ranches and towns. In the afternoon, they would have one-mile horse races, as well as games—including three-legged races—for the kids. In the evening, there would be a dance with music from banjos, violins (fiddles), guitars, mandolins, concertinas and

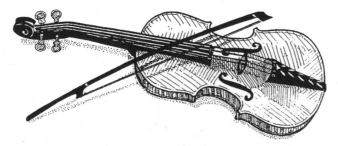

harmonicas. It would take a little time before all the musicians got used to playing music together, so that it sounded good. By the second or third try, though, everyone sounded fine. Even Uncle Frank would take his violoncello to play in the band; he would practice every evening until the night of the dance.

Someone needed to stay at the ranch while the others went to town and Frank asked for a volunteer. Charlie said he'd stay because he went to Elk Mountain for supplies once a month. Besides, he wasn't into getting all prettied up just to go to town.

On Friday night, Waldo made sure his saddle was polished and the bridle and reins oiled and wiped clean. He now was using a headstall and snaffle bit on Buck. The saddle blanket, he had washed at the river with soap and hung to dry over a willow bush.

Waldo got up extra early Saturday morning to brush and curry comb Buck so she'd look her best. Frank and Aunt Betty drove the wagon, and D.J., Chic and Waldo rode their horses. Everyone was dressed in the best of their well-worn clothes, which had all been washed, polished, mended and ironed to look as good as they could.

D.J. was looking extra sharp. He' donned a new light blue and white striped shirt and, over this, wore his fancy black vest. He had dusted off his hat and waxed the ends of his moustache to long upward curves that made it look like he had a set of long-horns under his nose.

When they rode into town, people were already there getting things ready. Older kids were helping the adults while the younger ones played catch-me-if-you-can.

Just as they passed Ox's blacksmith shop, someone called out Waldo's name.

Waldo looked and saw that it was Ashley Smith. "Ash," Waldo responded, "I haven't seen you in a dog's age. What you up to?"

Waldo rode over to Ash. "Step down and let's jaw a bit," Ash said. Waldo got off his horse to talk. "Let's go around the side of the building; can't talk over all that hammerin' of Ox's."

"You're lookin' more and more like a real cowhand, Waldo."

"What you been up to these days?" Waldo asked.

"I'm workin' a couple of days a week here for Ox cleaning out horse-apples from the stall in the livery, and anything else Ox needs doin'. He's payin' me two bits a week to help out."

"Doggone, that's more than you're worth," Waldo joshed. "Thanks a bunch," Ash retorted. "Hey, have you heard? The MacNeals are bringin' sheep into this here cow country?" Ash was always full of information because he lived in town and everyone he came in contact with had a new bit of gossip to share.

"No!," Waldo said, surprised.

"That's the word. The range is goin' to be full of those uglier-than-a-mud-fence critters."

By now, Wyoming had lots of sheep, and the sheep and cattle wars were already going on.

"I hear they eat all the grass, even the roots," Waldo said.

"Yeah, that's what they say alright."

"Uncle Frank will be fit to be tied when he finds out."

"Hey, the barn cat has a litter of kittens, six of them," Ash announced. "Want to see em?"

"Sure," Waldo said.

They went into the livery and headed to the hay loft.

"Hi, Ox! Hi, Alfonso!" Waldo greeted. "Ash is going to show me your new batch of monsters."

"You can have one if you want," Ox said. "There's too many for me to keep, and they're all weened now."

"I'll have to find out if it's alright first," Waldo said.

Waldo sized up the kittens playing with one another in the hay. He saw a nice-looking tiger kitten with a white bib. It was full of spunk. Ash grabbed it. "I think it's a boy cat, but it's too young to tell."

Waldo held the tiger kitten to his chest and it purred happily. "I do like this one!," he said, and then set the kitten down, he watched as the bow-legged cat walked off to rejoin the others.

"If Unc lets me have it and it's a male cat, I'll call him Cowboy cause he's bow-legged and looks like he was born in the saddle," Waldo told Ash.

Ash and Waldo walked outside again, and that's when Waldo saw a stack of wire spools on the boardwalk of the mercantile. "What's all that stuff in front of the Merc?," he asked.

"That's barbed wire," Ash answered. "It's used to fence off the range."

"Why?," Waldo asked.

"Don't understand it, but they say it's used in Nebraska and Oklahoma all over the place to keep everyone's critters off claimed land."

In 1876, Glidden barbed wire, along with many other kinds, was being used to fence off the West, and was killing open land.

"Dang it, that's as bad as sheep," Waldo said. "I'd better go find Uncle Frank and Auntie Betty."

Waldo told Uncle Frank and Aunt Betty about the kitten and asked if he could take it back to the ranch for a barn cat. Frank said yes, they could use a good mouse controller.

Later that morning, Waldo went over to Rasmussen's Mercantile to look at the rolls of wire. There were two wires twisted together with two sharp-pointed barbs along the wire every six or so inches. While he was examining the wire, his eye caught sight of something shiny between the large crack in the boardwalk. He got on his hands and knees and inspected it. Just then, Mr. Rasmussen came out of the store. "Vhat's you lookin' fur, Valdo?," he asked.

"I think I see a coin down under the boards here in the dirt. If I get it out, can I have it?," Waldo asked. Mr. Rasmussen thought if Waldo got it out from under the boardwalk, he would probably spend it in the store. "Sure," he told Waldo. Just then, someone came and wanted to buy something. Rass, as some people called him, went back into the store with the customer.

How can I get that coin out from between the cracks of the boards?, Waldo thought. He decided that if he got a stick and put some pine tar on it, maybe the coin would stick to it and he could pull it out. Waldo looked around and found a stick that would work. He went over to Ox's and asked if he could dip the stick into the bucket of pine tar he had there. Ox said sure.

Waldo went back and stuck the pine-tarred stick down between the boards. After a few tries, he finally got the coin to cling to it and he pulled it slowly up and out of the one-inch space between the boards. It was a small gold coin, as shiny as the day it was made because gold does not tarnish. He picked it off the pine tar, and discovered it was an 1891 $5 liberty coin!

Waldo couldn't believe his eyes, but quickly stuck the coin deep into his pocket and ran off to show Uncle Frank. Five dollars was a lot of money in those days—almost a month's worth of wages for a lot of people.

"Waldo, you're one lucky guy," Uncle Frank said. "But you did find it on Rasmussen's property."

"Rass said I could keep it if I got it out. I think he thought it was an Indian head penny, and I thought it was a dime."

"I suppose you're going to spend it right away."

"No, with the dollar I got for my birthday, I only need $4 more and I can order a .25-20 Winchester from Montgomery Wards, if you let me."

"Well, first you got to earn the needed $4, 'cause finding money is a thousand-to-one chance and that's slim-to-none odds, Waldo."

"I know," Waldo admitted. "Maybe I can make some lye and ash soap to sell, or trap a few beaver. I'll think of a way, plus I'm in no hurry to order the carbine anyways. I'll save my money."

By 2 p.m., everyone had eaten and the races had started. Waldo entered Buck in one race, and when the starter's shot rang out, Waldo spurred her and rode as hard as he could. He came in fifth out of twelve riders. He knew Buck wasn't the fastest horse, but they both did their best. "At least we weren't last," Waldo told Buck. "We gave them a good run."

That evening, after more eating, the music and dancing began. Waldo and Ash had never learned to dance, so they watched the goings on. Waldo showed Ash his gold $5 piece and Ash couldn't believe his eyes. "What you goin' to do with it?" Ash asked.

"I'm savin' it until I've got enough to buy a Winchester .25-20."

"What's it cost? A lot?"

"Yeah, $10.95 and shipping!," Waldo said.

"Why don't you get a larger caliber so you can hunt deer and elk?"

"Well, that's a good idea, but it might cost me a couple dollars more. I guess I could wait until I save more."

"You could get a .45-70, or a .38-56, model 1886, or even a model .92-44 with an octagonal barrel," Ash suggested. The night went on like that, the two of them talking about hunting, guns, horses and cows. They also talked about school, which was starting after the fall cattle drive that both Waldo and Ash hoped they'd get to go on.

After the celebration was over, most of the people stayed in town for the night and left for their ranches and homes the next morning.

Uncle Frank had heard the talk about the sheep and the barbed wire but said that he didn't let things get in the way of the once-a-year good time at Elk Mountain. He would worry some about it later, like all the others who didn't believe in fencing the West or watching sheep eat all the grass. Only time would tell all. This was his philosophy.

The kitten left its mother, brothers and sisters. It was on its way to the K Bar Ranch, riding inside Waldo's shirt with its head sticking out. It saw a new world in front of it, much different than the one into which it had been born in the livery stable.

It meowed for a while, but then settled down for a long nap, cozy and safe, enjoying the motion of Buck's walk to its new home.

That night at the ranch, Frank told Waldo he wanted to talk to him after supper.

"Waldo, you're pulling your own weight on this ranch, so I think you should get paid some for the work you're doin'," Uncle Frank said. "I'm going to pay you a dollar and four bits a month."

Waldo was surprised and glad that Uncle Frank thought he was worthy and good enough around the ranch to pull a wage like the men. And now he would, in time, get his own Winchester.

Chapter 9

THE DAYS were getting a bit shorter. The sun rose later in the east, set sooner in the west, and the nights got a little cooler. Now in September, the aspen and cottonwood leaves were starting to turn yellow. The geese were moving south from Canada and, in the early morning, you could see your own breath.

This was the time of year that the ranches hired waddies to brush pop the cattle in the aspen groves, round up all the steers, heifers, cows, and bulls for a head count, find any mavericks, and cut the yearlings and shippers out.

As in the past, the hands from the K Bar and Double X ranches worked together in the roundup. Waldo had to start school again, so he rode to Elk Mountain five days a week, and on the weekends he was hard at work helping out with the roundup work.

Frank Korn and George Sanders, owner of the Double X Ranch, had decided to drive the herd of market cattle to Cheyenne, over one hundred miles away, instead of taking them to Rock River, which was just thirty miles away. If they took their time and drove the herd around Sherman Pass to Cheyenne, they would get top money. Even though the cattle would lose a little weight on the longer trail drive to Cheyenne, prices there were so much

better than in Rock River that the cattlemen would realize a profit.

Waldo was to help on the drive and would have to make up his studies when he got back. Top hands were always hard to find, and every man was needed. Waldo wanted to become a top hand, a ramrod, and maybe someday a boss foreman.

Waldo rode the aspen hills, with Chic brush popping the cows out and onto open range toward the ranch herd, which was held together by out-riders.

Charlie prepared the chuckwagon for the drive. He rounded up the needed supplies—everything from large cans of Star pure lard, flour, and Blue Flame Coffee to Munsing long johns, which claimed to be perfectly fitting union suits. Charlie had mended the wagon canvas, greased the hubs, and rebuilt a set of brake shoes on the chuckwagon. He was going to be ready when it was time to move out.

Ash was asked to go on the drive as Charlie's campjack. Waldo was going to ride with the cowboys, keeping the shippers—the dry cows and steers to be sold to the eastern states for beef— moving east at a slow pace.

Ash, of course, wanted to go, and his father allowed him to do so. He wanted to see more than just the town of Elk Mountain, and could make up his school work with Waldo when they got back.

The stock was being separated; some yearlings, good, sound, young bulls and a good many cows would not go to market. Mostly, the fat steers would be sold. Frank didn't want Waldo to work the bulls, even though Waldo had the spunk and gumption to do so, because bulls were too mean and unpredictable. They might turn and charge the rider in a second, and they had been known to hook more than one horse and trample a few cowboys.

The drive would begin in a couple of days. The horse string had been wrangled and kept close. They were allowed to graze during the day, while being watched by the jinglers, and then put into the large corral at night. The corralled horses had to put up with the long-tailed, black, green and white magpies walking around on their backs looking for bugs. The horses would swish their tails over their haunches, making the magpies move off. And once the horses were turned out to graze, the magpies would fly off and jabber up a storm in protest.

The Double X shippers and horse string were now added to the K Bar stock. In the morning, the wagons were loaded and teams hitched. The one-hundred-mile drive was now under way. One thousand, six hundred and forty-eight head, not quite half from the K Bar, were being driven to the Cheyenne sales. It was a good year for everyone, and they knew the cows would bring in a decent return.

Waldo was assigned to ride drag along with other riders, one of which was Willie on his mule. The pungent smell of sage was in the air and, occasionally, a bunch of sage chickens would be startled in to flight away from the herd. The clouds created large splotches of shadow on the rolling hillsides. This had been a good year for rain, but now it was dry and the grasshoppers jumped in flight in all directions as the herd advanced. Fall was just around the corner.

It took four days to make it to Laramie and might take another four or five to get to Cheyenne. The herd had no problems crossing the Laramie River because it was shallow in most places. The herd was kept south of town because there was no way to get the herd over Sherman Pass, which was full of freight traffic and was heavily wooded.

During the drive, the string of cattle was sometimes more than a mile long. The point riders rode in front to head the herd in the right direction. On each side of the herd were the flank riders, who kept the cows from straying out of line. Drag riders generally were known to "eat dust" because they were at the rear of the moving herd. Nobody liked riding drag but everyone had to take their turn at it.

When noon chuck was ready and the herd stopped to rest, the cowboys took turns eating while others kept their attention on the cows. Cowboys rode into camp, ate their chow, rested, and changed horses for the rest of the day. Once in a while, a cowboy would ride in and not dismount; he would just sit in the saddle eating and drinking coffee while Ash dished food and filled cups for him. He'd take the plate and cups from him as he rode off to relieve another cow hand.

Having to move the herd south of Laramie meant following the Union Pacific Railroad tracks past a place called Tie Siding. This was a railroad camp where workers with broad axes hacked the logs flat on four sides, making railroad ties for the tracks to sit on. This was a very noisy place.

They kept the herd at least a half mile away from the tie camp, but the sound of the axes ringing out could be heard, nonetheless, in a continuous chime.

The nighthawks, who rode around the herd at night to keep the cows together and quiet, worked in shifts. While some watched over the herd, others slept. Even Waldo had to take his turn. Waldo would saddle a horse out of the picket string and take his turn nighthawking. This night, he relieved Cole, who had been in the saddle for almost eighteen hours. He needed some shut eye.

Waldo rode around the herd, making sure the cattle stayed together. The cows would moo occasionally, but rested, grazed and slept for the most part. Waldo could hear some nighthawks singing to the cows while another played his harmonica. He could see small, glowing red spots in the dark, which marked those riders smoking in the black of night. Nighthawking wasn't bad, just a little lost sleep. When the herd moved on the next day, sometimes a rider would drift to sleep, and someone would have to wake him before he fell out of the saddle.

Waldo liked nighthawking when the moon was out. He could see easily, as the moonlight reflected off the horns of the steers, and the singing of the cowboys sounded better than ever on these nights. He recognized Chic's voice as the one softly singing "The Night Herding Song."

"Oh, slow up, dogies, quit moving around. You have wandered and trampled all over the ground.

"Oh, graze along dogies, and feed kind of slow, and don't forever be on the go.

"Move slow little doggies, move slow—Hi O—Hi O—Hi O."

Another favorite song was "I Ride an Old Paint"

"I ride an old paint.

"I lead an old dan'.

"I'm going to Montana to throw the hoolihan.

"They feed in the coulees

"They water in the draw.

"Their tails are all matted; their backs are all raw.

"Ride around, little dogies, ride around them kinda slow, for the firy and snuffy are rarin to go. Ride a-rarin to go, etc..."

After breakfast, one of the foremen, or trail bosses, would give the orders for the day. "Right flanks—Frank, Russ, Kip, Cole, Waldo and Cal," and the next day, the order would be rotated. Riders exchanged horses every day in order to give them a rest, so Waldo didn't ride Buck all the time. This day, Waldo was glad to be on right flank because the wind was blowing the dust away from him. He saw a red fox dash from a den as the herd passed through a dry draw. The fox disappeared in a second.

The herd was driven across the two sets of railroad tracks, and headed in a straight line toward Cheyenne. This had to be done in a hurry because no one knew when the next train was coming. This was done in enough time but the hoodlum wagons—the bedroll and tent wagon—and chuckwagon did have to wait until the westbound train had passed before they could follow across. The train's engineer blew the whistle two long blasts in warning that it was approaching. This startled the herd, and some of the cattle started to run. Quickly, the cowboys turned the stock and bunched them up to keep them from stampeding.

"Son of a gun," Monte yelled. "I thought we were in trouble there for a minute."

Charlie and Ash had made noon camp by some large granite boulders that buffalo once used to rub on. This area was full of such large rocks. When Waldo rode in for his vittles, he jawed with Ash a bit. "How you handling the heifers?," Ash asked Waldo.

"Good! How you handling workin' with Charlie?"

"We work well together. He never yells at me if I mess up, and I'm not messing up now that I know what has to be done."

After Waldo ate, he handed Ash his plate and said, "See you tonight at camp." He mounted his horse and rode back to the herd, waving to Ash as he loped Buck in the direction of the herd.

That night was cold, and Waldo was glad he had gotten his gloves and Mackinaw out of the hoodlum wagon because even his union suit under his jeans and heavy flannel shirt would not have been enough to keep him warm while riding night watch.

At camp that evening, there was talk about the last two hard winters that had hit Montana and Wyoming. Lots of cows had starved to death and many a rancher lost more than half of his stock. By midnight, it started to rain and even snowed some.

On the last day before getting to the Cheyenne stockyards, the herd had been headed in a shortcut across a wet and muddy area. The mud was deep but Charlie didn't want to detour around this area. He thought the wagon and team could make it. The chuckwagon was almost halfway out of the mud when it got bogged down to the hubs and the team couldn't move an inch more. A few cowboys had to ride to the rescue. They tied their ropes to the wagon and, with their horses helping the team, they finally got the wagon out to drier land.

"Sometimes I ought to use better cow sense," Charlie told Ash. "I should have gone around."

South of Cheyenne, the herd again moved across the U.P. tracks and Crow Creek. They got to the stock pens and railhead at mid-afternoon. The men were glad that they would have the remainder of the day to rest from pounding leather. Even if a cowboy had a good circle horse, he was glad to be out of the saddle.

Cheyenne was parallel to the U.P. Railroad tracks, with the streets running diagonal to the main compass points, north to south. This was the city known for its Frontier Days Celebration, which had begun in 1897 and was the start of one of the first rodeos. Cheyenne became the Wyoming state capital in 1890.

The city was full of Army bluecoats, as they were called, plus Indians, dudes and dudeens from the East.

Everyone was glad to reach the end of the drive. Charlie was low in sowbelly (salt pork) and it almost looked like they might have to eat a slow elk. He had cut his food stores real close. Once relieved from the drive, though, many of the hands headed for cafes and saloons. Most of them just wanted to sit at a table and be served a two-bit steak and coffin varnish in a china mug.

Frank, Charlie, Ash, Waldo, George Sanders and a few others stayed in cow camp near the stockyards. A couple of guards were to take turns watching over the stock while the others rolled in.

The next morning, everyone showed up at the cow camp, except one of the waddies, an ex-soldier just a month out of the Army. He'd gotten into an argument with another poker player and both got red-eyed at one another to the point that there was shooting, and the waddie bit the dust. The killer had drawn and fired his iron before the cowboy had even pulled leather.

Frank and George haggled with the beef buyers until they got a good price for their cattle. When they had been paid, they, in turn, paid the men for their work on the drive. Those who wished or hankered to stay behind could, and those who didn't rode back to Elk Mountain with the remuda, chuckwagon and hoodlum wagon.

One evening, Ash and Waldo were talking to Chic and D.J. around the cookfire. As they looked up to the sky, it was lit up by the stars. They could see the Milky Way. They talked about how to find north by locating the Big Dipper. Chic pointed it out to Waldo, and Ash explained that the north star is the last star at the tip of the handle of the Little Dipper.

D.J. pointed out the Little Dipper and Hercules, and Ash

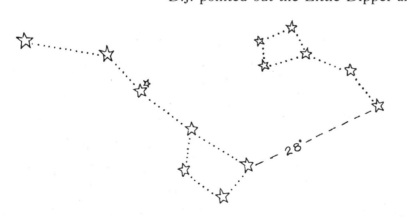

pointed to a shooting star in the east. It flew across the sky and then disappeared as suddenly as it had appeared.

The evenings at camp were very leisurely now that they only had the remuda to watch over. Everyone enjoyed these nights of relaxation. They told stories, sang cowboy songs, and played cards in the reflected light of the campfire and Charlie's lantern. Everyone was in good humor and great spirits.

Waldo talked to the cowboy who had loaned him the book, *The Last of the Mohicans*, and said he'd give it back to him soon because he was on Chapter 32. They discussed the book's heroes, Hawkeye and Chingachgook. The cowboy told Waldo that when he returned that book he would loan him his newest copy of the *National Geographic* magazine, which had an article in it about the fossil fields near Kemmerer, Wyoming. Fossils of millions of fish were found in the yellowish-white sandstone that once was the bottom of a large lake that covered most of the state of Wyoming, millions of years ago. Waldo couldn't believe that they were now camping on a site that once was covered by water.

"Even here, where we're camped?," he asked.

"Yep—all water," replied the cowboy.

They had made it back to the ranch in good time. Waldo was greeted by Cheyenne and discovered that the cat had grown bigger and had become an expert hunter of mice.

Waldo slept very soundly in his bed that night and awoke to the smell of coffee and sourdough pancakes with fresh eggs and bacon. He thought of how he loved cowboying but how nice it was to be home again. He was looking forward to going back to school in a couple of days. There was a lot to learn, and he wanted to learn as much as he could.

Chapter 10

ONE SATURDAY afternoon, Uncle Frank told Waldo to ride over to the Double X Ranch with a message for George Sanders. Waldo had finished the book that had been loaned to him so this was a good opportunity to return it. He also knew that he would be staying the night at the Double X bunkhouse, as it would be dark by the time he arrived.

Waldo dismounted at the hitching rail in front of the ranch as Mister Sanders appeared at the door.

"Howdy, Waldo. What's bringing you here at this hour?," he asked.

"Uncle Frank wanted me to get this message to you tonight. I guess it's important," Waldo answered.

"Come on in, and the Missus will rustle you up some grub," George said. "You just missed supper by an hour."

George Sanders was a man of average height, in his late fifties. He sported what is known as a saddle belly, more from eating well than from spending a lot of time in the saddle, even though he enjoyed both. He had mutton-chop sideburns and a moustache. Mrs. Sanders was still at the cookstove, a Windsor Range, canning wild chokecherry and huckleberry preserves. She said hello to Waldo when he entered the kitchen and asked if he had eaten before leaving the

K Bar. Waldo told her he had not eaten because he had left long before the dinner triangle had rung. He sat at the table while she made him something to eat. Waldo was hungry, and it was hard for him to keep from wolfing down his meal, but he managed to pace himself. He didn't want to seem impolite in front of the Sanders.

After Waldo had eaten, George asked him if he'd ever looked through a stereoscope. Waldo said he hadn't. In fact, he didn't know what a stereoscope was. Sanders brought one out of a box, along with some picture photographs mounted on cards. There were two photographs of the same thing on each length of cardboard. The cardboard was set in the wire slot on the stereoscope and, when he looked through the viewer, both pictures became one with everything appearing three-dimensional. Waldo was amazed at what he saw. The picture looked very real. Images in the foreground looked very close, and the background images appeared far away. Most of the photos were of Civil War series, since Sanders had been in the war as a young man, fighting for the Union Army. Waldo asked a lot of questions, and George explained the photos to him as he built himself a smoke. He was a heavy smoker and mostly smoked a brier pipe. He had many pipes, but on occasion he would roll a cigarette to satisfy his nicotine addiction. Mr. Sanders coughed a lot because of it, and Waldo thought to himself that he wouldn't get into smoking. It seemed to him to be a bad habit.

After he'd seen all the stereograph pictures, Waldo thanked George and Mrs. Sanders and went to the bunkhouse, where he found an empty bunk. He pulled his boots off with an old bootjack and rolled into his blanket for the night.

The next morning, he ate with the cowhands and tried the huckleberry preserves on some fresh-baked bread. It was delicious with

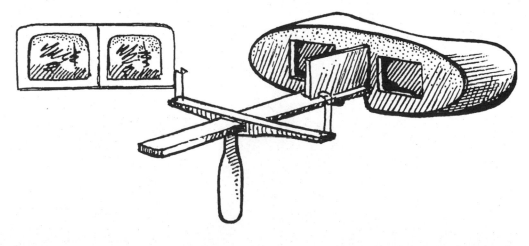

the eggs and ham—so good that Waldo had a second helping. Willie had smoked and honey-cured the ham.

Waldo returned the book and borrowed the *National Geographic* with its many pictures and interesting articles.

After saddling, he walked Buck over to where Willie was working. Willie was sitting at a foot-powered "Quick Edge" grinding stone, sharpening the splitting hatchet, axe, and kitchen knives.

"Howdy, Will," Waldo said. "That was the best ham I've ever had. You sure know how to cure."

"Glad ya liked it. Learned how ta do dat curin' in me youngin days," Willie replied.

"Well it sure is good eatin'," Waldo said. "See you next time, I reckon."

After shaking Willie's hand, Waldo swung into the saddle.

Willie went back to the grindstone and sharpening, and Waldo rode off waving.

Waldo was riding at a walk and had Uncle Frank's carbine out of the scabbard and across his lap in back of the saddle pommel. He was hoping to see some sage chickens. Chickens are good eating if you get young ones, he remembered Chic had told him. He shifted in his saddle. Just then, a large bird flew up ahead. Waldo reined Buck to a stop, looped the reins around the saddle horn once, and held the Winchester at ready. He watched the foreground and soon spotted some sage hens walking through the brush. Waldo took aim and fired at the head. Within a short time, he had four medium-sized chickens. Waldo tied the legs together and attached them to a back saddle string.

Waldo rode down into the willows of the Medicine Bow River to cross it, and headed upstream. The willows were very tall and thick in this area but there was a trail leading through them.

Suddenly, there was a great deal of thrashing in the willows. Waldo's first thought was that it was cows. He soon discovered, however, that it was a large bull moose rubbing his horns in the willows' growth. He hadn't gotten wind of Waldo's or Buck's scent, but there was no place for Waldo to turn Buck around. Buck's ears were up, forward and alert. Waldo decided to get Buck to back up slowly. He held the reins in both hands and tugged lightly at them.

Dammed if you do and dammed if you don't, Waldo reasoned, thinking of his predicament.

Once out of the brush, Waldo detoured and crossed the river further upstream. He didn't want any part of a bull moose in rut. Fall was an unpredictable time for bulls, as well as cow moose with yearling calves. You never knew how crosswise they will get.

A few miles from the ranch, Waldo saw a rider ahead and knew it was Chic by the way he sat on his horse.

"Looks like you shot some grub," Chic hollered.

"Naw! They just lost their heads when I rode in on them and asked what's cookin'?," Waldo joked.

Chic laughed and replied, "Good shootin'."

"I ran into a big bull moose in some willows and found myself in a fix," Waldo told Chic. "Didn't know if I should dig in my heels or bow my neck." Chic looked at Waldo with a wondering look.

"I guess you know I bowed my neck. He looked like he was full of spit and vinegar, and I wasn't goin' to call him windy," Waldo said.

"Yeah!," Chic replied, as they both rode toward the ranch. In the distance, they could hear the noon-chuck triangle ring out. "I remember once finding myself in a similar fix with a cow moose and her calf," Chic told Waldo. "They were grazin' in some willows when I happened to get in between them. She got so crosswise that she

charged me and my horse, Bandit, and if that old horse hadn't bolted with me pullin' leather, she'd have kicked us to the point where we no longer would be suckin' air." Chic liked stories that backtracked. "Heck," he went on, "someone would have had to come along and plant us, and we'd be pushin' up daisies now."

Waldo laughed but Chic looked serious just the same. Then he said, "I'll race you to the corrals!," and he sunk his spurs in his horse's flanks and bolted ahead. Waldo gave Buck his heels and a smack with his rawhide quirt on the haunches, and the race was on. They made it to the corral, neck and neck, before coming to a stop in a cloud of dust.

"Glad you could keep up with me," Chic laughed.

"I would have beat you but Buck wanted to graze before catchin' up to you," Waldo joked.

"We'll jaw about it after I get some beans in me, Waldo," Chic said. "Hope you didn't lose those prairie hens on that gallop."

Waldo looked back immediately to see if he had thrown his game away. He hadn't.

Aunt Betty was pleased to get the sage chickens, but Waldo had to pluck them after dinner so they could soak in salt water overnight.

By 8:30 that evening, Waldo was ready to hit the hay. On his way to bed, Uncle Frank told him that since D.J. and Chic were off Sunday, he'd like it if Waldo could ride south to the head of Turpine Creek and Cortex Creek. Waldo was to see if he could find any of the herd in that area. If so, he was to try to round them up and bring them down to the low land. At the ten-thousand-foot level, there might be a few bunched critters up in the high meadows, and this would give Waldo a chance to scout the areas where the elk might be as well. If he got a chance, he'd drop one, as D.J. and Chic would be around to help pack it out the next day—that is, if the bears didn't get to it first.

"By the way, Waldo, you better not take that moocher, Cheyenne, with you because he'll run off the elk, and if you do get one, he'll eat up what he shouldn't," Frank said. "He'd leave nothing for the bears and prairie lawyers. Better take along some spare rope and a sharp knife too."

"I reckon I'd better start right after chores," Waldo said.

"Make sure that the carbine's good and clean," Frank reminded.

"It is," Waldo answered. "I took care of that first thing after pluckin' the hens."

Waldo went to the door and whistled for Cheyenne. The dog came in to sleep at the foot of Waldo's bed, as he did every night. Waldo noticed Cowboy out by the barn, crouched down in position to spring at something in the grass. He jumped at it and came up with a mouse in his mouth, and then headed for the barn to eat it.

Waldo thought if they had a milk cow he'd give Cowboy some milk every day, in turn for his hunting down the rodents. But then he remembered that having a cow would mean another daily chore for him, so he decided that if he got an elk tomorrow he'd save Cowboy a bit of liver as a reward for his hunting skills.

The next morning, Waldo went out to the horse yard and wrangled the horses, including Buck, into the corral. He slipped the gate poles back into place so the horses wouldn't get out. He then put the headstall, bit, blanket and rig on Buck.

D.J. and Chic appeared with their ropes to catch their mounts. D.J. put his silver inlaid Las Cruces bit and horsehair headstall on his horse. He only used this fancy gear when he went to town. Waldo moved Buck out of the corral and to the hitching post in front of the house, and then headed to the kitchen for biscuits and gravy.

Laughing loudly, Chic and D.J. entered a minute later. By this time, Frank was on his third cup of coffee.

"What's so funny?," Frank asked.

"Walt Hoffman's goin' to double harness today with a mail-order bride from back East. She's such a dudine, I don't think it'll last through the winter and cabin fever," D.J. said, still chuckling.

"Yeah, I heard," Frank said with a smile as he looked at his wife. "Only time will tell—and a long Wyoming winter. If they make it through this one, there'll be another in six months to savvy one another in. Hope it's not like the winter of '87."

The winter of 1887 was one of the worst and the longest in Wyoming and Montana history. That winter killed thousands of cows, horses, sheep, and wild animals.

"Well, Chic and me been invited to this shindig," D.J. said.

"I reckon we'll be able to kick up our heels," Chic chimed in.

Charlie said he was sorry for Walt's tenderfoot squaw.

After breakfast, the hands excused themselves and thanked Mrs. Korn for the morning vittles.

"Great sop and hot rocks," D.J. complimented.

"We better vamoose," Chic told D.J. "Sun's breakin and we're burnin' daylight."

"See you later, Charlie," Waldo said, as he put the carbine in the scabbard and stepped in the stirrup. Sundays were Charlie's day for meditation.

"Remember," Charlie said, "if you take an elk, give thanks to it for giving its heart to you."

"I wouldn't forget you teaching me that," Waldo said. "Its heart line, I will breathe into it."

Waldo rode off telling Cheyenne to stay. Cheyenne stayed put until Waldo was out of sight, and then went off to look for Charlie.

Frank and Charlie had watched Waldo ride off.

"Waldo's makin' a hand, a darn good hand," Frank said. "He's got the love for it; he's never beefin' and never lets anythin' gnaw at him."

Charlie nodded in agreement. "He's got what it takes. He'll run some outfit one day, maybe, or at least be a right-hand man."

Waldo rode along Turpine Creek until the high coulee banks vanished. Now in the forest, there was a light breeze and the sun was still warm. The few golden leaves still on the aspen trees fluttered, and some blew off and floated to the ground.

Having ridden another five miles into the high timber, slowly making his way around and over deadfall lodgepole pines, Waldo saw signs that the cattle were in the area and maybe, he thought, just up ahead.

Waldo rode up the ridge and away from Turpine Creek. He was at the head of it. The creek was dry by this time of year and would stay dry until it snowed. The pine needles on the forest floor made Buck's steps nearly noiseless, until she hit a hidden rock with her iron shoes. The clink seemed to echo loudly over the countryside. When they reached the top of the ridge, Waldo was able to see a large meadow. To the southwest of it, he could see a herd of forty or more elk. They were in the shadow of an island of pines. He could see their breath, especially when one of the bulls let out a bugle—"Whoo-eeeeeeee!" The sound made Waldo's hair stand up, and his skin had goose bumps all over it.

The herd was made up mostly of cow elk and calves, but in the group were also many large bulls and a few spikes.

He moved Buck back and out of sight from the herd. He dismounted and pulled the Winchester from its scabbard. He looked over the ridge at the herd. Some were grazing, while others lay resting in the grass. The bulls kept their eyes out for unexpected danger. Waldo knew he would have to move in closer to be in range to shoot.

Afoot now, he took his time, moving slowly and as quietly as he could. He had left Buck tied to a smooth tree with a halter and a lead rope. He tied her short so she wouldn't get herself into trouble by moving around in the timber.

He kept low whenever he thought he might be seen by one of the bulls. Finally, when he figured he was in range, he checked the herd again. It was much colder this high in the forest and, where the sun no longer shone on the northern slopes, there was a skiff of snow that wouldn't melt until late spring. Waldo could see his own breath now. He'd worked up a sweat sneaking up on the elk. Now he rested for a minute, so as to catch his breath and settle his heart from the excitement. He checked the direction of the breeze by wetting his finger and holding it in the air. The wind was from the southwest and would not carry Waldo's scent to the herd.

He looked at the herd again; there was a bull looking in his direction. Waldo froze in his tracks.

He didn't move a muscle. When the bull went back to eating, Waldo moved into a good position, leaning against a tree for a steady aim. He let his breath out, then breathed in and held his breath. The bull was sideways to him, and Waldo's sights were on the animal's heart. He felt himself shaking a little, not from the fear of the animals, but from the fear of killing such a magnificent living thing. He let out his breath again, breathed slowly in, let half of the air out of his lungs, held it and squeezed the Winchester trigger. A shot rang out—loud as thunder! The entire herd sprang into action and bounced like a herd of stampeding cattle being turned by cowboys. They crashed downhill into the safety of the heavy timber.

Four mule deer Waldo hadn't seen also took off in another direction, away from the rifle shot. This all took but a second, and Waldo stood looking where he had aimed. He could see nothing. I must have flinched, he thought. He was perplexed. In a way, he was glad he'd missed and yet angry that he had shot so poorly and was not as good a hunter as he had thought. He started walking ahead to see if he'd wounded the elk. He was going to look for spots of blood on the ground, until he saw the bull's antlers sticking up in the tall grass.

Waldo remembered what Charlie had once told him: When you come upon game you've shot, be very careful, as it may not be dead and it could kill you. It will fight for its life and you must always be ready to fight for yours.

Waldo pulled at the lever of the Winchester, ejecting the spent cartridge and putting a new load in the chamber. The bull lay dead where he had stood only moments ago. Waldo kept the barrel of the gun pointed at the bull. Then he saw the bullet hole and the puddle of blood on the ground.

Waldo looked at the lifeless eyes becoming dull, losing their brilliance by the second. He put his head down to the bull's nose and drew its breath. He stood, his carbine hung at his side, and tears rolled out of his eyes. This was not like shooting a sage chicken, he thought. Shooting a sage hen was very impersonal, but killing an elk hit home.

Waldo knew now that he never wanted to be in a predicament where he would have to shoot a human being. He turned and walked back to Buck, and relieved the hammer of the carbine out of the firing position.

Two hours later, after much work and with elk's blood up to his elbows, Waldo had completed the job of gutting and quartering the animal. He looked around and saw a small marshy pond not far away. Waldo walked to it and found a place where the animals had come to drink. Here he washed the blood off his knife and hatchet, as well as his hands and arms.

Waldo had gotten the quarters up off the ground, over some dead-fall, so the meat could cool down and not spoil before the pack horses could carry it out.

When Waldo walked back to Buck, her ears were up and her eyes were wide open. Waldo had to talk her at ease because she could smell the blood from the elk. She sunfished around for a bit, and when she settled down, Waldo saddled up. Buck sidestepped a little and Waldo almost blew a stirrup.

Waldo noticed that the sky was turning gray, and he was getting cold from the chill in the air. He untied the Mackinaw from behind the cantle and put it on. He rode Buck down the west side toward Cortex Creek. When he reached Cortex, he swung north again and toward Turpine Creek, keeping west of it this time.

It started snowing very lightly, melting as soon as it landed on Buck's head and body. But just a short time later, the snow was coming down heavier and building up on the ground. Waldo gave Buck her head by slackening the reins and letting her find her own way back down the mountain. He remembered Chic telling him, "When in doubt, let your horse do the thinking." She picked her way over the now snow-covered deadfall. Waldo's ears were feeling the cold. He pulled his Mac collar up to protect them. Buck had made her way out of the timber and onto a meadow where there were bedgrounds and five steers. Waldo couldn't see their brands because of the snow on their backs.

He rode up to them and kicked them up and moving. Buck and Waldo headed them toward the ranch, knowing that once he got them down with the other stock they would stay there because of the snow that had built up to six inches by now.

About seven miles more and he'd be back at the K Bar. He'd eaten some jerky and a couple of cold biscuits and he wished for some hot coffee but it was still a long way to the ranch kitchen. The snow kept falling steadily, and Buck now was wearing snow on her head and haunches. They finally made it to the main herd and turned the five cows loose to join them.

Waldo was tired and very cold when he got to the barn. Chic and D.J. saw him come in and Chic told him to go on in and chow, and that they would unsaddle and grain Buck before putting her out with the other horses.

"Thanks," Waldo said. "I got a bull elk up top at the head of Turpine Creek. And I ran five steers back to the main herd."

Waldo detailed the day's experiences to everyone. He didn't brag about killing the elk. And he didn't tell anyone about his tears, except Charlie, whom he told later that night when they were alone.

Charlie assured him that it's fine for a man to understand life and death, that we all mourn the going over the Great Divide with tears, and that some folks hide the tears better than others, but they still have them. He asked Waldo about the breath, and Waldo told him he had taken it.

Cowboy got a slice of elk liver the next morning. The five yearlings Waldo had found were mavericks.

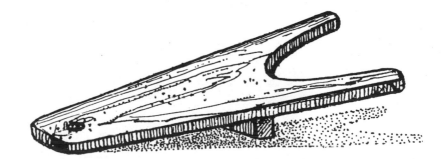

Chapter 11

WITH TWO packhorses, Chic, D.J., and Waldo in the lead, they moved through the eight to ten inches of new snow to the high meadow above Turpine Creek. The frozen elk lay quartered and up on some deadfall, covered in a cold white blanket.

Both D.J. and Chic had packhorse experience, as Waldo did from the last fall deer hunt. The pack animals had sawbuck pack-saddles with the lash and cinch, and sling ropes plus manties tied to them.

When they got there, the sun was beginning to warm up just enough that the snow was starting to melt.

There were signs that a bear and coyotes had argued over the gut pile. The bear had won but the coyotes had taken the four legs and hooves to eat. The bear also had gnawed at one of the hind quarters. Aside from that, the elk meat was in good shape. Waldo had roped the elk's horns up in a tree.

On one of the packhorses, they slung the front quarters—the right quarter on the left side of the horse and the left quarter on the right, with the ribs out and the elk horns lashed down over the two slung sides, the antler beams in the cavities of the ribs, and the tines to the rear so they were not likely to stab the horse or catch on anything while moving through the trees or brush. It took everyone's help to do the job quickly. Chic and D.J. fastened the lash and cinch to hold the loads. The second packhorse carried the hind quarters slung upside down and inside out and lashed to the horse and packsaddle. Waldo held the horse while it was being packed and watched how the two men used the slings and lash to secure the cargo.

Chic led one packhorse down, and Waldo led the other with the load of hind quarters.

"Waldo, this is a nice six-point bull you shot!," Chic exclaimed as the group came out of the timber and headed up the Medicine Bow River. Waldo nodded but said nothing. Trailing behind each other made conversation difficult. Besides, Waldo's mind was on the dead elk.

Waldo had to make up that Monday's school work since he'd missed the day packing out the elk. That night, he studied late.

October just slipped by, as did the snow from the early storm, for now the ground was dry once again. But the high mountains held the cold air and snow.

The November mornings seemed to get colder; the frost was thicker and so was the ice in the horse trough. Even the edges of the river had iced up. The aspens and cottonwoods had long ago lost their golden leaves. The sun rose much later in the morning and set earlier, making the days shorter. Winter was setting in for its long stay. Waldo did a good many of his morning chores by the light of a lantern when there was no moon to see by. It seemed like the half hour before the sun came into full view was always the coldest time of day.

Waldo hadn't let Aunt Betty cut his hair since August because

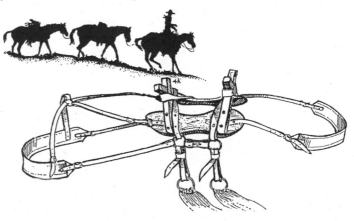

he wanted it to grow over his ears through the winter to keep them from getting frostbitten. Chic and D.J. now were using their woolly chaps, or angoras, as they were sometimes called, to keep their legs warm while riding long hours in the Wyoming cold.

Charlie had been busy making sure the line shacks had ample food supplies. Everything that the mice might get into was kept in glass jars or in large tin lard cans.

Line shack number one was a sod hut with a grass-covered roof and two glass-bottle windows. This line shack, built into the hillside, was located near a spring east of the K Bar. This area had very little wood near it, so Waldo and Charlie made sure there was an adequate supply to make it through the winter. It was a small place and easy to keep warm with the wood stove. The walls were sixteen inches thick, and the dirt floor was rock hard from the many years of being wet down and swept.

One Friday afternoon after Waldo returned from school, Uncle Frank told him to plan to ride to the Shooting Iron Ranch with a message as soon as he finished his chores the next morning. This ranch was at Cedar Pass, a long distance south of the K Bar.

When Waldo awoke, there were six inches of new snow on the ground and it looked as if it was there to stay. It had stopped snowing but it was still clouded over. Waldo knew that the snow would be deeper as he rode closer to the mountains en route to the Shooting Iron Ranch.

The ranch had the reputation of being a tough outfit. Old man Austin Kincaid, who had once run a ranch in Texas, decided to start his own spread with thirty head of cows and settled in this area of Wyoming. Though he'd built up a sizeable cow herd, he had more horses—the best breeding stock around.

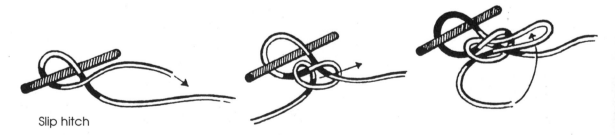

Slip hitch

The ranch crew was made up of four men—Austin, in his seventies; his sons, Carroll and Emmet, in their fifties; and a Chinese cook called Ling Chew, as old as the rest of the crew. Old man Kincaid always packed two Remington six shooters, and was still a dead shot, even at his age. One of his revolvers had five notches on the grips. "Men that got in me way got kilt," he was once heard to say. Those in the Kincaid clan were thought of as jayhawkers. It was said they had sent many a man to Boot Hill. If they knew you and liked you, however, you would be given the shirt off any of their backs.

Waldo arrived at the long, low, log ranch house just at dusk.

Austin was at the door with his double-barrel shotgun in his hand and both six guns at his waist in the cross-draw fashion. The light from the lantern at his back created a long shadow to the front of him.

"It's me, Waldo! From the K Bar!," Waldo shouted.

"Well, well, well. What brings ya here at this hour, Waldo?," Austin asked while pointing the barrels of his shotgun toward the ground, then politely opening the breach and extracting the two brass shotgun shells. "Come on in and git warmed up. Ling, put his horse up an feed et some oats." Waldo dismounted, and gave Buck's reins to Ling. He was stiff from the cold and came into the light and warmth of the log cabin.

"Gettin' to be winter out there," Waldo said. "I came to bring you this letter from Uncle Frank."

"We're just sittin' down to vittles and I know you're probably hungry as a bar."

"Yeah, I am," Waldo replied as he sat down at the table. Emmet gave him a blue and white metal enamel plate with what looked like

Clove hitch

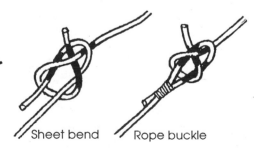

Sheet bend   Rope buckle

Quick release knot

some sort of stew and a chunk of hard bread, along with black coffee.

During dinner, Austin was in one of his storytelling moods and was reminiscing. He told Waldo and the others, who had heard these stories a hundred times, about the time when he helped drive cows from the Belle Fourche River in the Black Hills of Dakota Territory west across Wyoming and Montana—the Bozeman Trail, it was called. He talked about Col. Charles Goodnight, one of the kings of Texas cattle drives north. "I've pushed beeves ever since I was knee-high to a grasshopper," he said, "and that's why I like horses better. Besides, a man afoot is no man at all!"

After dinner, he lit his pipe and kept chatting while Ling went about doing the dishes. Carroll and Emmet had disappeared and Waldo, who was very tired, politely listened to Kincaid's stories.

"Ya know how we ended up with horses in this here country?," he asked Waldo.

Waldo said he didn't know, but guessed that there always had been horses here.

"No, no, no," Austin said. "The Spaniards brought horses here. Not until 1621 were the Pueblo Indians allowed to have horses. After the 1680 Pueblo Revolution, the Indians stole Spanish horses and sold them to the Comanches in turn, making them Lords of the Plains. By 1750, the horse was clear up into Canada. By 1770, all Plains Indians in the West had horses. Prior to that, the Plains Indians moved by following the buffalo herds, using dogs to carry their possessions on travois made of tepee poles."

By 9:30 p.m., Austin noticed that Waldo couldn't stop yawning.

"I reckon you're bushed," Austin said. "Besides, et's late and time to hit the hay."

"I'm glad you told me about the horses and all," Waldo said. "I enjoy learning about things."

"Well, you're welcome to any of my storyin' any time. You'll take that bunk in the corner there," Kincaid told him. "You can use that buff robe to keep the cold off your bones if the fire goes out."

Before daybreak, Ling was milling about and, within minutes, had a fire going and the coffee on. Waldo rolled out of the bunk and from under the heavy buffalo robe that had kept him so warm all night.

After breakfast, Austin Kincaid gave Waldo a letter for Frank Korn. "Waldo, you should have some woollies on those leg bones of your'n. And since you don't, I'm going to let you have an old pair that been around here forever," Austin said. "They used to be Carroll's, but he up and got new ones sometime ago."

"I'll go git 'em out of the tackshed," Carroll said.

"No need to do that," Waldo said. "I'll be fine."

"Son," Austin said, "when a Kincaid says he's givin' ya somethin', take et, et's yours."

Carroll came in with the old black woollies and Waldo put them on. They were a bit too long but, once in the saddle, they would rise up to the correct length. Waldo couldn't believe his eyes.

"Don't like warin' black no more so I had white ones made up two years ago," Carroll said. "I ain't wore these old things since. Like Pa said, you're welcome to em."

Waldo thanked them and said if there was anything he could do for them, he'd be more than happy to.

"Maybe someday, Waldo," Austin said. "Stay warm."

Waldo could feel the difference. The bone-chilling cold was not cutting into his legs as he rode north.

The day was very quiet, with no sound except Buck's footsteps. The landscape was white and the trees ahead looked like tall black giants against a gray sky.

Waldo was easily able to follow his old tracks from the day before because no new snow had fallen.

He made pretty good time riding up and down the mountainous terrain and was close to getting out of the timber, when he rounded a bend and Buck's ears perked up—just as Waldo spotted a large black bear. Buck came to a sudden stop, and the bear charged. Buck turned from the trail and, with Waldo hanging on to the apple, or horn, bolted away from the bear.

By the time they reached the edge of the wood, Waldo had lost a stirrup and the reins. Buck was not going to stop. She leaped over some deadfall, and Waldo lost his grip. He hit the ground hard. The wind was almost knocked out of him, but he still managed to get up and look around to see if the bear was coming. Fortunately it had lost interest in the chase. But Buck was headed home without Waldo.

Waldo kept walking. Maybe she'll stop and wait for me, he thought. After what seemed like hours of walking, Waldo could still see Buck's prints in the snow—but there was no horse in sight. Even with only ten inches of snow, Waldo's feet were getting cold, though the rest of him was hot and sweaty.

Sometime later, he thought, he'd have to make camp and get a fire going. He had just three hours of daylight left. Waldo built a lean-to out of boughs from a fir tree and found some dry deadwood to make a fire. He had a good pile, enough to make it through the night, he figured. Waldo made a tepee for kindling. He reached into his Mackinaw pocket for the strike-anywhere matches he'd put there. They were wet. He must have gotten snow in the pocket when he fell off Buck. Looking them over, he found one that looked dryish. He struck it with his thumb nail; it hissed and caught fire. Waldo's hand was cold and his fingers stiff, shaking as he put the match to the pine needles. The match went out. He tried the others he had, but no luck. Damn, he thought, Buck, I'll shoot you if I freeze to death.

Wiggling his toes in his cowboy boots and putting his hands under his armpits, he tried to make himself comfortable for the night. He lay there in the lean-to thinking he should not stay there without a fire, that he ought to keep moving. He ached all over and was tired.

Suddenly, he thought he heard a noise. He listened. Could it be a bear? Was he dreaming? Then he heard it again, coming his way. Waldo looked out from his shelter and there in front of him stood an Indian on a mousy blue-gray colored grulla horse. The Indian had Buck's reins in his hand and Buck behind him. Waldo scrambled out from under the shelter. The Indian made the sign of greeting to Waldo and Waldo answered with a "Howdy!"

"You lose horse, I find. Maybe I keep," the Indian said using sign language as he talked. Waldo didn't know what to say. He hadn't seen very many Indians, at least no wild ones—only those that hung out in Laramie and, of course, Charlie.

This mounted Indian was young, about the same age as Waldo. He was wearing dark blue wool-blanket leggings with stripes of beadwork down each leg and a white Early's Witney Point blanket copote. There was a bow and quiver full of arrows hanging on his back and, across his lap, an old 1866 Springfield .45-90 rifle with a brass-tack design and rawhide repair work on the stock.

"Yes, I lost my horse; a bear spooked her," Waldo told the Indian. "My name is Waldo Sparks. What's yours?"

The Indian dismounted by slipping a leg over his horse's head and sliding down to the ground. "I'm Six Feathers," he told Waldo, as he handed him Buck's reins.

"You make good camp. No fire?," Six Feathers said. "Much wood."

"I got all my matches wet and couldn't start a fire," Waldo explained.

Six Feathers set his rifle down against the shelter and pulled out a small leather packet. "Strike a lite, make fire," he said. Inside the pouch was a piece of iron, a chunk of flint and tinder. The Indian got down close to Waldo's stick tepee. After striking the steel to the flint a few times, sparks smoldered in the small amount of tinder, which he blew on until it ignited. Then he put it to the pine needles. A fire at last!

They picketed the horses that night. Six Feathers and Waldo kept the fire going and took turns sleeping in the shelter. Six Feathers told Waldo that he was a Shoshone. He had left the Wind River Reservation in his quest for the return of the buffalo. As he talked to Waldo the next morning, Six Feathers would occasionally slip from English to Shoshone and always used sign language. Waldo would say he didn't savvy and Six Feathers would repeat what he'd just said in broken English.

Waldo had given Six Feathers a piece of beef jerky and a biscuit that was in the saddle bags. Six Feathers pulled out another buckskin bag and brought out a small catlinite pipe bowl and wood stem. He loaded the pipe with Kinnikinnick—bearberry leaves and other herbs and the inner bark of red willow. Before taking a

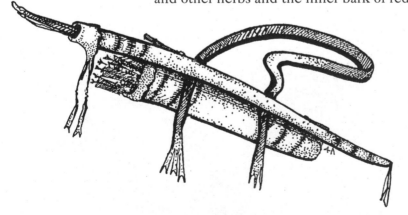

puff from the pipe, he pointed to the four sacred directions of the medicine wheel and handed Waldo the pipe. Waldo took a puff himself and handed the pipe back. Though he was not a smoker, Waldo did this so as not to insult the Indian. He didn't inhale the smoke, but he made believe he had and then let it out slowly like he'd seen D.J. do with a coffin nail.

Waldo asked him about the large-caliber rifle he had, and Six Feathers told him that he had taken it from its cache in a dry cave. It had belonged to his father and he had kept it hidden for when the buffalo returned.

Waldo asked if he had seen any buffalo on his travels from the reservation, and Six Feathers had said, no, he had seen only sheep, cows and a few horses.

"Buffalo all gone. I go back to Fort Washakie. Do sundance so buffalo come again next spring—when dog star rises," he said.

"I've only seen a couple of buffalo once," Waldo told him, "but that's when I was a boy in Oklahoma."

"We need buffalo to hunt again. Arapaho eat dog. Shoshone never eat dog. We need buffalo meat, not white eyes cows' meat."

Together they rode from the lean-to camp north to the K Bar. Waldo owed his life to this Indian that had returned Buck to him and helped him.

Six Feathers was made to feel at home at the Korn Ranch. When he left for the Wind River Reservation, Aunt Betty made sure he had plenty of jerky, bacon, bread and a jar of chokecherry jam.

Waldo wished and hoped that Six Feathers would have good weather on his trip home, some two hundred miles away.

Six Feathers later became an Indian police officer in the Wind River Reservation.

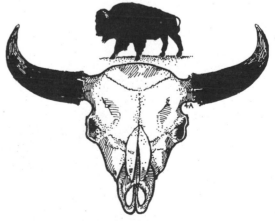

Chapter 12

WINTER WAS here for the duration. New snow had piled on top of old snow that had fallen a week ago. It was to be hoped that the winds would blow and clear large areas of grassland for the cows to graze. The herd needed to be watched and moved to new clear areas from time to time. Winter was the most worrisome time of year for the cattle raisers. Cattle don't migrate from one area to another like the buffalo used to do. Horses fare the best in winter because they will dig through the snow to find feed and, in the worst of situations, they have been known to eat willow bark and the young growth.

Chic was holed up for his winter stay in the sod line shack number one, and D.J. was living in the log line shack number two, near the beaver ponds. Both of the line shacks were east of the main ranch. The line shacks to the west, north and south were occupied by cowhands from bordering ranches, and everyone kept a close eye on the welfare of each other's stock. Helping one another was the strength of ranching in those early years.

Chic made sure he had plenty of tobacco, lamp oil and a large variety of long, differently colored horse hair. He spent most of his nights in the line camp braiding horsehair, making all sorts of good-looking horse trappings. He made bridles, reins, hat bands, hobbles, belts and a half a dozen other things from colorful horsehair. Chic had been collecting horsehair for many months, pulling the hair from the tail and mane. Hair from the mane is softer. He had washed and bundled each type and color into neat long bundles and stored them in a clean flour sack. White horse hair was always a problem for Chic to get since white horses were few and far between.

D.J. Faiths prepared for his winter stay in the log shack by stockpiling as many books and periodicals as he could beg, borrow and buy. He also made sure he had plenty of lamp oil and firewood. Night came early and, without sunlight, the bitter cold followed. The long night was spent partly hugging the stove, cooking, reading or repairing tack before hitting the sack.

The mornings in the line shacks started when the hands rose, checked out the weather, and rebuilt the fire in the stove if it had gone out during the night. They would use the fire to make coffee and cook some bacon and leftover beans and to heat wash water to wash and shave, if they didn't care for a winter beard. If the weather looked good enough to ride, the cowboy saddled one of the two horses stationed at the line shack, and made a circle cruise of the stock. Ice at the water holes and river's edge was chopped out enough so the horses and cows could drink. Even if the animals ate snow, it was never as good as a good long drink of cold water.

On snowy and windy days, the cowboys stayed in the cabins. Many cowhands who had decided to be out in bad weather got lost and froze to death. Sometimes they died only a few feet from the shelter of the line shack during a whiteout. The winter got so

bad at times that going from the barn and back to the ranch house was impossible without a rope strung between the two to find one's way in the blowing snow.

Thanksgiving had come and gone, and the fall jamboree in Elk Mountain had been as pleasant as the summer picnic. Frank Korn held a long meeting of the ranchers at the schoolhouse. The men all left late and with long faces, and Waldo wondered what it was all about.

Some days later, Waldo and Ash talked about the meeting. Ash had heard that it was about fencing off ranch lands in order to keep the sheep out. The bleating sheep were moving onto the winter cattle range and eating up the winter feed. There was real concern that if there was another hard winter, a lot of cattle would be lost to starvation.

"They're talking about getting water to the fields near the river and then cutting the grass in the fall so cows will have feed come winter," Ash told Waldo.

"Heck, how they expecting to get the water to the fields?," Waldo wondered aloud.

"I don't know," Ash said, "but this arm's starting to bother me some. Wish I hadn't broken it."

"Well it's a good thing Doc Elliot was in town that day 'cause I don't think he could make it in this deep snow with his fancy new Studebaker wagon," Waldo said.

"Doc said it's better to have it splinted up in the winter than in the summer, 'cause it shouldn't itch as much in the cold."

"Ever since the sawbones hung up his shingle in Wilcox," Waldo said, "people have been getting hurt or think they're sick, Uncle Frank says."

"Well, I'm glad he was around to set this arm," Ash replied.

"How'd you manage to break it just by jumping out of the loft anyways?," Waldo queried.

"I hit it on an open stall door when I landed on the floor," Ash explained.

"Will it be back to normal by Christmas?," Waldo asked.

"I sure hope so!," Ash sighed.

Frank Korn had made his fall catalogue order by the middle of November. The usual arrangements were made with the bank in Cheyenne to pay for the order and freight when it came in from Chicago, Illinois, by train. In this Montgomery Ward and Company order of Frank's was Waldo's order for the Winchester he had decided upon—a model '92 repeater with a round barrel in a .44 caliber. Waldo managed to save up the money he needed, and also ordered a box of ammunition. In addition, he ordered Christmas presents—a hand mirror for Aunt Betty and a cattleman's pocket knife for Uncle Frank.

It was early December, and Waldo already missed not having D.J. and Chic around. Charlie and Frank took care of all the ranch work, with Waldo's help on weekends. Waldo had missed four days of school due to a major snowstorm that came roaring in like a mountain lion and brought two and a half more feet of snow. Frank Korn was worried about this storm but, just one day later, a good wind came up and blew a lot of snow off the range, exposing the dried grass for the stock. Though the winds were good to have, it made that day unbearable for man and beast to bear. The stock had moved to the lee slopes to find what little shelter there was, and they kept their backs to the wind all day. It was so cold the cows just stood with their backs hunched up and their heads down.

The next day, Waldo helped Uncle Frank move the horses and bulls from one area to another, where the feed was more plentiful.

Freight wagons now were traded for freight sleds that traveled from the railroad towns to outlying areas. Most of the travel to town was no longer done by wagon but by square box cutter or wagons with carriage runners attached to the four wheels.

Aunt Betty was always baking since the cookstove was going day and night. She made bread, as usual, every day, and on Wednesdays, she baked pies. Sometimes they would be meat pies and sometimes berry pies, but the peach pies with the canned peaches were everyone's favorite.

One weekend, Waldo asked Uncle Frank if he could visit Chic, and Uncle Frank told him yes, because there wasn't anything pressing to do around the ranch.

"Take Chic the letter that came for him," Frank said.

"And take him three loaves of bread and a meat pie," Aunt Betty added. "But don't eat it on the way, Waldo."

Waldo knew he'd have a good time visiting Chic because Chic was always telling stories. Waldo woke early on Saturday and went about his chores in the pre-dawn darkness. By the time he wrangled Buck, the sun was burning away the morning frost, but the air was very cold and would stay so all day. The frost crystals were so thick in the air that they created a vertical rainbow as the sun shone through them. The smell of woodsmoke was strong in the freezing air. It hung low in a horizontal line, floating very slowly from the chimney to the east. The snow was noisy under foot and cracked with every step.

Waldo hitched Buck to the O-ring in the barn, and then hung

the oats bag over her nose and let her eat while he went in for his breakfast and coffee.

He then rode off with two blankets rolled up in his slicker and tied to the back of the cantle. The bread and pie were in a sack tied to the saddlehorn. Cheyenne watched Waldo ride off. "Come on Cheyenne, let's go visit Chic," Waldo called out. "We'll camp the night at his fire." With an excited bark, Cheyenne ran to catch up.

On the way, Waldo saw some of the cows—along with a few antelope does and yearling fawns—eating the dry grass on a windswept area. Farther on, he saw three coyotes traveling together and marking their territory.

When they reached the sod line shack, only one horse was in the corral. Chic was out checking the stock. The latch string was out in the door, so Waldo walked in. It was warm inside, and there was a pot of coffee sitting on a flat rock atop the stove to keep it warm, but not boiling. Waldo looked in the wood box and saw that the kindling was low, so he went outside with the axe and began splitting wood.

Chic rode up, and Waldo turned around just in time to catch him building a loop.

"I thought you was a wood thief makin' chopsticks out of good firewood," Chic laughed at Waldo.

"You wouldn't lay a loop over me while I had an axe in my hand, would yah?," Waldo joked back. "I'd have chopped your reata into a lot of little two-foot-long lariats for you."

Chic put his horse in the corral. "Let's have a cup, Waldo. I've got to warm my feet. Thanks for makin' up some kindlin'."

Inside, they sat next to the stove. Cheyenne came in and lay near the heat of the stove while he licked the ice from between

his toes. Chic built a smoke after pouring each of them a cup of coffee. As always, Chic put a lick of sugar in his coffee.

"What's in the sack, Waldo?," Chic asked.

"Oh! Aunt Betty had me bring you some bread and a meat pie."

"Let's have a piece of pie with this coffee," Chic said. "I didn't mess with eatin' anything this morning and I'm starved now!"

"It's probably stone cold," Waldo said.

"Heck, I'll just set a couple pieces on these metal plates and put 'em on the stove for a few minutes before we dig in."

Cheyenne's eyes were now on the plates. He knew Chic would set his plate on the floor after he finished eating and let the dog clean up what he missed.

After eating, Waldo set his plate down for Cheyenne to lick up too, since Aunt Betty wasn't around to frown on him for doing so.

"Cheyenne looks like he could be a top-notch skillet-licker," Chic joked. "With him around, one don't need to do dishes."

After an hour, Chic and Waldo saddled up and cruised north to check the stock. Chic stopped to examine one of the cows that had cut itself on something and had an ugly-looking gash on its right shoulder. Even though the puncture was covered in blood it was not serious and the wound would heal on its own.

They got back to the shack two hours before dark and unsaddled the horses, grained and hobbled them and set them out to graze for the night. They grained the second horse, but Chic kept it corralled so he'd have a mount to jingle with in the morning.

"It's too soon since we ate to start eating again," Chic told Waldo as he stoked the fire and added a couple of logs. "We'll heat up some more meat pie after dark."

Chic lit the lamps so they would have a little better light, and then sat and started braiding horse hair. Waldo watched as Chic's fingers sorted out the different-colored strands.

"How'd you get into hitchin' horse hair?," Waldo asked.

"Well, since you asked, I reckon you should know. I spent a year in a Chihuahua prison in Mexico on a mix-up. I was bushwhacked by some hombres. Then I was accused of havin' stolen someone's saddle. Anyways, being a gringo and not speakin' much Spanish at the time, they railroaded me into prison with no evidence. That was the longest fourteen months in my life and, if it hadn't been for Benito, who was doin' five years in the same cell as me, I'd have died of boredom. Benito was one heck of a horsehair hitcher," Chic went on. "I remember the first time I tried braidin'—what a mess! But in time, which I had plenty of, I got the hang of it."

"Here, try your hand at it," Chic said, handing some to Waldo.

Waldo took some horsehair and tried, as Chic explained what was what and how to hold and pull the strands of hair as he braided.

After dark, they took a break from braiding and had some chow. Chic was telling a story about the time he and another cowhand ran into a herd of twelve or more javelinas, or peccaries as some call them.

"I tell you, these here little pigs was runnin' through the cactus and mesquite. Well, we got the idear to rope a couple and after we finally got them in the open, I tossed a loop over one's head. Choco heeled another by the back legs. Of course, both pigs went berserk. Our ropes got crossed, pigs squealed and horses started buckin'. We had a good old wreck. My pig ran off with my rope and Choco had to shoot his pig in order to get his rope back.

"There was no other way to get around the trouble we got ourselves into," Chic continued. "Heck, those javelinas just about tore us up once we were afoot. Our dead ends was full of cactus spines."

"What happened then?," Waldo asked, laughing.

"We licked our wounds, caught our ponies after a while, and had roast pig for two days' chow," Chic said. "I don't ever want to try that trick again. They're as bad as ropin' a bear, only smaller. Right after that, Choco and me started workin' for the Diamond Bench Ranch."

The next morning, Waldo awoke to Cheyenne wanting to go out. Chic woke up at the same time and got the stove fired up. They had some oatmeal mush with a splash of molasses on it and a cup of coffee. This was morning chow, as Chic was not much of a cook.

Waldo had managed to make a small watch fob with red, white, and black horsehair. The braided fob was nice and uniform and Chic complimented Waldo on his good workmanship.

They rode the circle together that morning, checking the cows and moving them to an area that was windswept on higher ground, with grass exposed. There was a light breeze blowing, which made it colder, even though the sun was shining. At noon, they rode back to the line shack and had coffee, plus what was left of the meat pie. Waldo washed the dishes while Chic went out and split wood after building a smoke.

By nightfall, Waldo and Cheyenne were back at the ranch. For the last mile, Waldo put Buck into a canter to keep warm. He had the watch fob he'd braided in his pocket, and thought he'd give it to D.J. for Christmas.

One evening in the middle of dinner, D.J. showed up at the ranch. He was already starting to suffer from cabin fever. He needed to be around people sometimes. Waldo told D.J. that he should take the cat back to the line camp with him for company. D.J. was delighted with the idea; besides, he was having a lot of problems with mice, and Cowboy would put an end to that. Waldo also said that if it was all right with Uncle Frank, he'd ride over to the line shack and spend the weekend with D.J.. Frank didn't see any reason why Waldo couldn't ride there, as long as something didn't come up.

D.J. stayed in the bunkhouse with Charlie that night and left for the cabin with Cowboy under his coat the next morning. Cowboy wasn't too thrilled with the ride and wanted to jump out and vamoose back to the barn. D.J. had to hold on to him good to keep him from escaping. D.J. was glad that he had a leather vest on under his coat, because Cowboy's claws were digging into him. Back at the cabin, D.J. gave Cowboy some liver from a deer he had shot for camp meat two days before. After he made the fire in the cabin stove and things began to warm up, Cowboy settled with the idea of staying for a while. He found a good spot on D.J.'s bunk to wash and sleep.

Waldo awoke to a clear, calm morning. The trees and bushes all had a half inch of frost on each twig and branch, and the temperature was well below zero. As Waldo walked out to the barn, the snow crunched underfoot. He could feel the cold instantly coming through his boots. This morning, he was going to visit D.J., but Cheyenne didn't want to go because it was too cold on his paws.

Waldo put Buck's bit under his coat and held it up against his arm pit to warm the metal before putting it in Buck's mouth. After saddling his horse, he rode off toward D.J.'s line camp. He was taking with him a couple of old newspapers, bread, and a batch of sugar cookies for D.J.

The saddle was cold and it squeaked with Buck's every step. Waldo kept wiggling his toes in his boots trying to warm them. He rode light in the stirrup and had all his weight on the saddle seat because his feet were so cold. He had a scarf covering his ears under his hat, and he kept his left gloved hand tucked inside his Mackinaw and would switch rein hands when his right hand got too cold.

When he got to the line shack, D.J. was inside. Waldo dismounted stiffly.

"You look just about froze to death," D.J. said, coming out of the shack.

"Aw heck, I'll be good as new once I get my feet warmed up," Waldo told him.

"Wish I had some red chile stew," D.J. said. "That would warm your innards. But I haven't seen hide nor hair of a chile pepper since I got north of the Canadian River. Go on in and warm yourself; I'll take care of your hoss for you. She's gettin' a good thick winter coat on, looks like."

Waldo took his boots off and just about set his feet into the stove box to get the feeling back into them. When D.J. came in, Waldo was still bundled up and his stocking feet were starting to steam.

"Better move your feet from the stove. Ya goin' to get them burnt up."

"They don't even feel warm yet," Waldo said.

"Take your socks off and massage your feet and toes with your hands to get the blood flowin' in them again. You'll be fine in a couple of minutes," D.J. assured. "Ya get those feet workin' again and we'll have a cup of mud and some of this deer meat stew. I made it with a couple of spuds and an onion. Sure wish I had some chile peppers to give it a kick, though," D.J. added.

"My feet are starting to tingle," Waldo said.

"Good, that means the blood's movin'," D.J. replied.

Waldo's feet and the rest of him warmed back up to normal shortly.

"I didn't think ya'd bother comin' on such a cold day," D.J. said.

"Well, I told you I'd be here," Waldo said. "Wasn't you expecting me?"

"Thought you had more sense to know not to ride on such a cold day."

"You'd have rode out to see me if it was the other way around."

"Now you're the pot callin' the kettle black," D.J. told Waldo.

"Maybe. How's about some of that stew you're cookin' up?"

Cowboy jumped off the bunk and stretched, yawned, walked over to Waldo and sprang onto his lap.

"Cowboy! I forgot you were here. I had my mind on getting warmed up and not much else. What are you feeding this cat, D.J.? He weighs a ton."

"Deer meat and anything he spots movin' around here. He's gotten a pair of chipmunks and a batch of mice. And if he ain't eating, he's sleeping. But he's been nice to have around to talk to. He even talks back when he gets a mind to."

"Come an get it!," D.J. said as he dished up some stew.

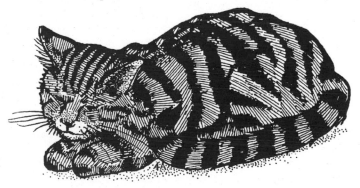

"Good stew, but your coffee's really mud," Waldo remarked.

"It ain't mud. I just make it thick," D.J. smiled.

"That's a gooder, thick," Waldo said. "Any thicker and it wouldn't be a liquid anymore."

"I don't know what you're hootin' an' hollerin' about," D.J. said. "You drank it."

"I chewed it 'smore likely and swallowed it in chunks," Waldo laughed. D.J. handed Cowboy a piece of stew meat from his dish and said, "You give some people peaches and cream, but all they see is a dirty dish."

"I'm sorry D.J. I didn't say it was bad coffee, just mud," Waldo joked.

"Here, have a sugar cookie to dunk in your mud," D.J. shot back.

"Well, I'll tell ya one thing I know, and that's that I'm not cruisin' the beefies today. They're on their own in this cold," he said as he put another log in the stove.

"The ones I saw comin' in looked all right, just haunched over from the cold," Waldo said.

That afternoon, it hadn't warmed up any. It was going to stay bitter cold. D.J. and Waldo moved more firewood into the cabin, given the horses oats, and Waldo brought his saddle inside and gave D.J. the old newspapers to read.

D.J. would read the papers and then, what he didn't use as T.P. and fire starter, he turned into wallpaper. He had mixed flour and water to make a paste and spread it on the newspaper, then glued it to the cabin walls. This served to cover the cracks in the logs and keep the cold air out and the heat in. He had two coats of wallpaper on all the walls, and was starting a third layer now.

Some old cabins had as many as six or seven coats of paper on them, and had even been whitewashed.

Looking up from his reading with Cowboy, who was now on his lap fast asleep, D.J. said, "I suppose you read this thing here in the paper about that English duke up in Sheridan hunting elk with his fancy hounds."

"Yeah, I remember reading it," Waldo said.

"Well, that reminds me of the old three-legged hound that the boss had on my first ranch job back in Texas. This dog was called Spook. Anyways, the ole man claimed Spook got to snooping around some lobo (wolf) bait and got his front left leg caught in a steel-jaw trap. When someone found him, the dog had just about gnawed his own leg off.

"The ole man loved that hound," D.J. continued. "You'd better never say anythin' bad about it without gettin' chewed out and havin' to listen to him tellin' ya how smart this dog was. I remember him tellin' someone that ole Spook was so smart that the dog could bark from both ends," D.J. told Waldo, laughing.

"That musta been some dog," Waldo chuckled.

"Yeah, but most of the time he just laid around in the shade and gnawed or scratched at his fleas."

Later that day, D.J. and Waldo played a few games of checkers, using a checker board drawn on the table top with a lead bullet and the odd squares blackened with charcoal from the stove. They used two different caliber bullets for the checkers and, when it came to kinging, they put two bullets next to each other and moved them both as needed.

Sunday was as cold as Saturday had been. D.J. told Waldo to keep the stove fed with wood while he did a quick cruise of the stock. Waldo said he'd ride along, but D.J. told him that he had a long ride to the ranch that afternoon and that there was no need for him freezing to death twice in the same day.

D.J. didn't waste any time in the cold. The cows all looked miserable, with frost on their haunches. He rode through the herd and then headed back to the shack to warm up. He walked in carrying his saddle. Icicles had formed on his moustache, and his nose and cheeks were red from the cold.

"I hope we get a bit of snow soon just to warm things up," D.J. said to Waldo. "It's too cold for man or beast out there."

"We need a chinook," Waldo said.

"We only get those at the end of January or February, if we're lucky," D.J. added.

Waldo rode off that afternoon, after saying his goodbyes to D.J. and Cowboy. The sun was shining but the cold remained. If it had warmed up at all, he couldn't tell.

Christmas was only a week away and Waldo was looking forward to it. Everyone would be at the ranch, and Aunt Betty's cakes and cookies would be plentiful. There would be a Christmas tree, a big dinner, presents, and a good time for everyone.

Chapter 13

IT WAS three days before Christmas, and Frank Korn took the cutter into town to pick up the large Montgomery Wards order that had arrived at the mercantile. Waldo told Uncle Frank the order had arrived; he was excited because he knew the Winchester had come with it. Waldo suggested that he take the cutter into school and pick up the merchandise, but Uncle Frank had some business to take care of in town anyway.

Charlie had been at Elk Mountain getting supplies the same day the order had come in. Unfortunately, he had headed back to the K Bar as the freight sled arrived in town from the opposite direction. They just missed one another by a few minutes. Charlie had taken the axe with him and made a short detour to a place Waldo had told him of, where he had seen a nice spruce Christmas tree. He cut it down with two swings of the axe and put the tree into the cutter.

Waldo had planned to cut the tree down and drag it home with his reata, but Charlie told him he was going to town with the cutter and would get the tree. When he returned to the ranch, he set the tree in a snow pile until Christmas Eve, when they would take it into the house to decorate it.

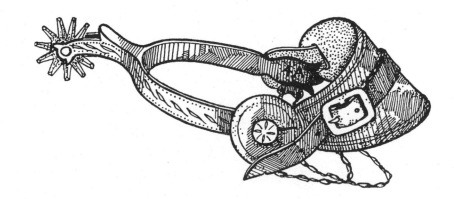

Before riding off from school, Waldo rode over to Rass' Mercantile, with Ash walking alongside. Ash's arm had to stay in the splint and sling for a while longer, Doc Elliott said. "Time's the best doctor," he had affirmed.

"Howdee Mister Rasmussen, and Merry Christmas!" Waldo and Ash said, as they entered the Merc.

"Merry Christmas to the both of you too!" he replied. "I suppose you came in to see if the Montgomery Vards order has been picked up?"

"Yup," Waldo said.

"Your Uncle picked it up, but he left vithout these four tins of peaches he vas to take home. He got to talking to George Sanders after loading the cutter and plumb forgot. I vas vith a customer when he drove off vithout the tins."

"I'll take them home; I know Aunt Betty wants to make peach cobbler for dessert on Christmas," Waldo said. "Can I borrow a sack to put them in?"

"Sure, here you go!"

"Much obliged," Waldo said, as he and Ash walked outside.

"Ash, I better skeedaddle on home with these peaches."

Ash knew Waldo really wanted to see his new carbine. "I've got to go do chores myself," Ash said and waved goodbye to Waldo with his good arm.

"Merry, merry Christmas, Ash!," Waldo shouted as he rode off.

"A merry one to you too, Waldo. Hope you let me try shootin' some tins and bottles with your new gun."

"You bet!" Waldo hollered back.

Waldo gave Aunt Betty the peaches, which she was glad to get as she had been worried that she wouldn't be able to make her favorite Christmas dessert. Canned peaches were hard to get and expensive in the Old West. They were considered items for special occasions only.

"You saved the day with the peaches, Waldo," Frank said. "I plumb forgot about them.

"Oh, I put your carbine on your bed," he added. "You better get it out of the case and make sure it's what you ordered."

The Winchester was well-packed in a rough wooden case and wrapped in an oiled cotton cloth setting in straw packing to protect it in shipping. Charlie brought a hammer in from the barn, and everyone watched as Waldo pried the nails out of the case. The Winchester smelled of gun oil. The walnut stock was dark, and there wasn't a scratch on it. The metal was a polished shiny black. Waldo worked the tight lever while pointing the barrel to the ceiling to make sure there wasn't a cartridge in the breach. It was a habit he had learned from Uncle Frank.

"Always check and make sure to see if the gun's loaded," Frank had insisted. "More folks get a bad surprise when they think it's not loaded. They end up shootin' a foot or their horse by accident. You should treat all guns as if they were loaded, even if you are told they're not." This was a wise lecture that Waldo followed whenever handling a gun.

"It's sure stiff," Waldo said as he inspected it.

"It will loosen up once you've shot a box of fifty rounds out of it," Charlie said.

"Yea, that will put the soft in it," Frank seconded.

"Waldo, my only words of warning are never ever point a gun at anything you're not sure is what you intend to shoot to kill," Aunt

Betty said. "I remember once when this boy shot his younger brother thinking he was a coyote in the raspberry bushes. All his cryin' never made a bit of difference; his brother was still dead." And she dropped the subject and went back to the stove to check on dinner.

After wiping it with his bandana, Waldo put the new carbine on the gun rack next to the other guns. He stepped back and looked at it with content.

By noon on Christmas eve, D.J. and Chic had arrived at the ranch. They put their horses up and went to the bunkhouse to take off their snow-covered wooly chaps. After shaking the snow out of the chaps and hanging them up, they went to the main house for some hot coffee. It had been snowing lightly all morning, so the cold snap was over for a while.

D.J. had started to let his beard grow out, and it made him look very sinister until he smiled. Chic thought of letting his grow out but he couldn't get used to it, so he managed to shave at least every other day.

As usual, Aunt Betty was cooking and baking while Waldo, who had just returned from the root cellar, was peeling potatoes and carrots in the kitchen when D.J. and Chic walked in.

"Merry Christmas," everyone wished one another. Frank had ridden out to check on the horses and Charlie was at the coop culling a couple of chickens for Christmas Eve dinner.

"Waldo, you're goin' to be the best biskit shooter in the whole state as much time as you spend in a kitchen," Chic said.

"Well, you can peel some of these spuds if you're into learning how to cook," Waldo answered, smiling.

"No, thanks, " Chic replied. "When I have to cook, I just burn it until I know it's not goin' to move, or I eat it raw."

"That's because you don't have any taste," D.J. said. "So I'll just eat your share of peach cobbler since you couldn't tell if it was charcoal or hay you're eatin'."

"You should talk, D.J.; you can't even cook coffee, and that's just boilin' water."

"Well, at least Waldo likes my coffee. He told me so," D.J. said.

"I bet!," Chic uttered, shooting a doubting expression at Waldo. Waldo just laughed.

"You men pour yourselves some of my coffee and have some sugar cookies," Betty told them.

Throughout the rest of the day, everyone continued kidding with each other. Even Frank and Charlie got in a few joking punches. Everyone laughed at one another; and even though it might have sounded like there was a serious side to the joking, it was all done in fun and not meant to hurt anyone's feelings. It's just that everyone knew each other's peculiarities.

The spruce tree was set up on a stand. It had a makeshift paper star as a finial and was decorated with garlands of red rose hips and white popcorn, while paper loops linked together to make a chain. The ornaments were made from ginger and sugar-cookie dough.

There were only fourteen or so small candles waxed to the ends of branches and ready to be lit after dark. It was a small tree, only seven feet tall. But it sure looked pretty with the candles lit that night, Waldo thought.

Waldo showed off his new Winchester with pride.

"I suppose you're broke now," D.J. accused.

"Yep, sure enough," Waldo answered.

"Broke is what happens when you let your yearnins get ahead of your earnins," Chic chimed in.

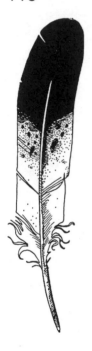

"Heck, you earned the wages," D.J. said. "Might as well spend it on a good Winchester than on rye whiskey snake poison."

"Yep, it sure is a good-lookin' shooter," Charlie interrupted. "Who gets to put the first round through it?"

"We'll draw straws tomorrow to see who," Chic said. "We could shoot some tin cans and bottles from the dump if we can find any under this snow."

"It's Waldo's carbine and he earned it; he'll put the first round through," Frank corrected. "You boys have had more new things to christen in your past than Waldo has."

Nobody was going to argue with the boss, and it was late, so the men wished everyone a merry Christmas and a good night and headed to the bunkhouse. The snow had stopped and the stars had come out. Frank and Waldo blew out the candles on the tree. And Waldo and Cheyenne turned in.

Waldo woke up early Christmas morning. He and Cheyenne hurried out into the cold crisp air. Waldo got his chores done quickly and was at the wood pile when Charlie came up to help get a load of wood inside.

"I'll take the aspen in," Charlie said. "I'm dyin' for a cup of coffee."

Aunt Betty was taking biscuits out of the oven when they walked into the kitchen.

She thanked them for the wood, and told them to help themselves to some coffee. "It looks like a great Christmas day," she added.

"I'll help with the cookin'," Charlie told her. Chic and D.J. came in with a couple of presents wrapped in newspaper and tied with string. They put them under the tree with the other presents.

After breakfast, Waldo helped do the dishes while Frank and the hands talked.

After a while, they opened the presents. First, Aunt Betty opened Waldo's present to her, which he had wrapped in a piece of white butcher paper and tied with a narrow red ribbon. She loved the hand mirror. Uncle Frank got a double-bladed spring-back pocket knife from Waldo. And Waldo was surprised to get a pair of steel spurs with polished and chased design, buttons and double-heel chains. The rowels had twelve points, and there were set-in drop shanks with chap guards. These were from Uncle Frank.

He also got a corduroy vest, which Aunt Betty made for him. It was a great Christmas for everyone. Waldo had given D.J. the horse-hair watch fob, and D.J. had given him a paisley neck rag. Chic had given Waldo suspenders, and Waldo had made a set of spur straps for him. Waldo gave Charlie the two ivory tusk teeth from the elk he had shot, and Charlie presented Waldo with a nice eagle feather he had found under a roost and saved. Waldo knew the feather was something Charlie believed to be strong medicine. He would tie it to the side of his hat.

"Lets see how you shoot, Waldo!," D.J. exclaimed, after the gift-giving was complete.

Everyone except Aunt Betty and Charlie went out to the dump. They kicked around in the snow until they found six or seven tin cans and a few bottles to balance on a rail section of buck fence against the hillside.

When the tins and bottle targets had been set up, everyone moved back a hundred and fifty feet. Waldo looked at the Winchester.

"Let's see you knock that blue magnesia bottle to smitherines," Chic told Waldo.

Waldo aimed at what looked like a small blue bottle the size of a penny from that distance. He shot but the bottle just stood there.

"A sure way to land in Boot Hill is to shoot without aimin'," Chic said, everyone knowing full-well that Chic was the worst shot in the bunch.

"Here, see if your shootin's any better," Waldo challenged, handing Chic the carbine.

Chic wished he'd kept his mouth shut, but aimed at the blue bottle, shot and splintered the rail, unbalancing the target so that it and a can next to it fell into the snow.

"Now that's shootin'—two for the price of one," he bragged.

"But the rail's not the target," D.J. joked.

Everyone had a chance to shoot the new gun and all agreed it was a good shooter and not a ditty. They had finally shot all the bottles and tins, including the magnesia bottle that Chic reset on the rail and Frank shot to bits.

By mid-afternoon, Christmas dinner was ready. Everyone enjoyed themselves and ate so much that they were stuffed to the point of bursting.

With Cheyenne running ahead, Waldo and Chic took a ride after dinner. They needed to move around to ward off sluggishness that accompanied their full stomachs. Sporting his new spurs, neck rag, suspenders, and vest, Waldo felt like a million dollars. A hawk with its white winter plumage flew low over them. He nudged Buck with the spurs lightly and she sprang into a gallup. Snow flying from her feet, she almost ran over Cheyenne, who jumped out of the way just as Waldo slowed Buck to a lope. Chic caught up.

"What's the all-fired hurry?," Chic asked. "What got her to feelin' her oats?"

"I just tickled her with my new spurs," Waldo laughed. "That sure woke her up!"

"I guess ya got a top hoss under ya."

As they rode back, Cheyenne took off chasing a jackrabbit and was long gone for a while. In the willows down by the river, a coyote hunting a mouse had its ears up and its head cocked slightly. Suddenly, it leaped into the air and came down head-first into the snow. A second later, it was chewing down a rodent for its Christmas dinner.

"Now, that's how Cheyenne should hunt, instead of losin' weight runnin' all over the range at top speed and comin' up empty-handed," Chic laughed.

"He just needs to work off tallow after Christmas dinner," Waldo added.

Further on, they saw two mule-deer does with three yearlings bounce out of the riverbottom and over a snowy hill top.

It had been a great Christmas Day for Waldo; everyone had shared a wonderful time.

The New Year was around the corner, and Waldo now was thought of as a cowboy by everyone, a hired hand on horse back. Winter would pass and spring would bring green grass, sandhill cranes, newborn calves, colts and fillies. Calving would have him busy, as he would help D.J. and Chic pull the calves into the world when cows were having difficulties with breech births and were in trouble.

The roundup, cutting, roping, riding the circuit, and working the colts to ride were all part of the good, hard-working life that Waldo loved. He knew, and he wanted to be a cowboy forever.

A fix - Trouble.

Arbuckle - Adjective applied to a cowboy, implying that the boss must have gotten him by mail order with Arbuckle premium stamps.

Backtracking - Talking about old times.

Barefooted - Unshod (horse).

Bear sign - Doughnuts.

Bed roll - The blankets and bedding owned by each cow puncher; they are usually rolled up with a tarpaulin around them.

Beefing - Complaining.

Bend - To turn a stampede or a general movement of animals.

Biscuit shooter - The cook.

Bite the dust - To die.

Blow - v. To lose a stirrup while riding. Also, to let a horse stop for breath in high altitudes.

Bogged down - Trapped in a swamp or bog. Sometimes used when a person is 'swamped' with work.

Bogging them in - Holding a tight spur in the animal's belly.

Boot Hill - Cemetery.

Bounce - v. To turn animals (see 'bend').

Bow your neck - Give up your convictions.

Broncho, bronco - Loosely, an untamed horse.

Broom-tail - A wild mare.

Buckaroo - Cowboy or bronc buster.

Build a smoke - To roll a cigarette.

Bunch quitter - An animal that strays frequently.

Bunkhouse - The place where the cowhands live.

Bushwhacked - To wait and capture or kill someone from behind a hiding place.

Santa Barbara bit

Las Cruces bit

Glidden barb wire

Bootjack

Angora chaps

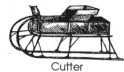

Cutter

Cabin fever - Sick of long winters and having to spend too much time inside.

Cache - Hiding place.

Cache - v. To hide.

Campjack - One that helps out the cook and sees that the camp is kept in order.

Cantle - The rear part of a saddle.

Cavvy - String of horses used in ranch work, such as roundups.

Chaps - Short for Chaparejos: leggings worn by cowboys for warmth and protection when riding in brush.

Chinook - A warm wind from the south, named for the Chinook Indian.

Chow - See grub.

Chuckwagon - Kitchen on wheels that follows the roundup.

Circle horse - A good horse with the stamina to cover territory in roundup.

Coffin varnish - Liquor.

Coffin nails - Cigarettes.

Conchas - Metal ornaments adorning saddles, chaps, bridles, etc.

Cord of wood - A cord is four feet by four feet wide and high and eight feet long. It weighs 2,000 pounds, or one ton.

Corral - Enclosure in which stock is confined.

Coulee - Bed of a stream, even if dry, when deep and having inclined sides.

Cribber - a horse that has a habit of gnawing on wood, such as corral rails or hitching racks.

Critter - Animal.

Crosswise - Mad.

Cut-horse - Horse used to cut out animals from a herd.

Dally - v. To 'take a dally' is to circle the rope around a post (snubbing post) or saddlehorn in order to hold a roped animal.

Deadfall - Dead trees that have fallen to the ground.

Dewlap - A strip of hide cut and left hanging under an animal's neck, for identification purposes. Also, called wattle.

Dip - Strong antiseptic to kill lice or scab on cattle or sheep.

Ditty - A new tool or contrivance or practically anything unfamiliar to the cowboy.

Dogie (also doughbelly) - Motherless calf that trails behind the herd and causes endless trouble.

Double harness - Get married.

Drift - n/v. Animals 'drift' in a storm away from their regular feed grounds.

Dude - An Easterner or city person new to the West.

Dudine - Feminine of dude.

Dug in your heels - Stuck to your convictions.

Fan tail - Wild horse (or broom-tail), so called because their tails grow long—fanning out or dragging the ground. Wild horses have no one to cut their tails for them.

Fancy gear - Trappings, i.e. bits, spurs, chaps, saddles, etc.

Fork a hoss - To ride a horse.

Goin' callin' - Going courting.

Grabbin' the apple - Grabbing the horn of the saddle to hang on.

Graze - To eat grass.

Grub - Food, vittles or chow, chuck, bait.

Grulla - A gray horse with stripes on its legs over black socks and a dorsal stripe down its back. Also called a Zebra Dunn.

Flint and steel

Hackamore - A halter of rawhide, braided and snug-fitting.

Half-shot - A term applied to a person who has been drinking.

Hand - A working cowboy/cowhand.

Hang up a shingle - Business sign made of wood.

Haze - v. To ride at the side of an obstreperous broncho in an effort to keep the horse from running into a fence or some obstruction. Term used in breaking horses.

Hazin' - To move animals out of the brush.

Hit the hay - Go to bed.

Hobbled - To tie both fore legs.

Hold up - Men in line camp in winter. Nevertheless, they don't exactly stay "holed up," as there is plenty of work to do.

Rawhide and
leather hobbles

Hondo - Leather or metal loop at end of lariat.

Hoodlum wagon - A second wagon used in the roundup for carrying the extra beds and bringing wood.

Horse wrangler - Man who brings in the horses each morning from the range or out of the night herd.

Hot rocks - Biscuits.

Branding Irons

Iron man - One who keeps the branding irons hot at branding time.

Jack - Male mule.

Jaw - To talk.

Jayhawkers - People not much for being on the side of the law.

Jinglebob - To split the ear of a steer or cow to the head, letting the pieces flap.

Jingler - Man who takes care of cavvy.

Kick up your heels - Dancing.

Kinnikinnick - Indian tobacco.

Javelina, or peccary

Lariat - Rope (also called 'string').

Lasso - Spanish for reata.

Latigo - A strap for lacing saddle on.

Lick - A spoonful of molasses, sugar or honey.

Line rider - Man employed to ride and repair fences. In the days of the open range, men rode an imaginary line and turned their cattle back from it.

Makin' a hand - Learning to become a full-fledged cowpuncher.

Man-killer - A vicious horse that will kick, strike, and bite.

Maverick - An unbranded calf or critter (derived from family name of Samuel Maverick of Texas).

Moocher - An animal, usually a pet, that hangs around dooryard and barnyard, eating anything it finds.

Moon-eyed - A horse with white, glassy eye or eyes.

Mule - A mule is conceived when a male donkey (jack) is mated to a mare. Mules can live to 25 or 30 years old.

Lariat

Naw - Something bothering you.

Nice kitty - A skunk.

Nighthawk - Cowboy on duty at night.

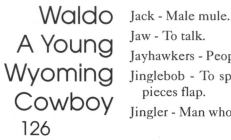

Pack saddle frame

Oklahoma rain - Sandstorm.

Onery - Recalcitrant (mean) horse or cow.

Pack saddle - Framework especially designed for pack animals.

Packhorse - Horse trained to carry a pack.

Pilgrim - A newcomer.

Pinto - A spotted pony.

Poke - Savings of money.

Pound leather - To ride.

Pounding leather - Means to be in the saddle for a long hard ride.

Prairie lawyers - Coyotes.

Pull leather - To draw one's gun from its holster.

Pulling leather - Holding on to saddle with the hands.

Rake - To scratch a horse with spurs, or drag the spurs along his neck, to make him buck.

Reata - Also called lasso, a cowboy rope made of rawhide that is braided or twisted or manilc, hemp, Mexican magney, sisal and, nowadays, nylon fiber.

Red-eyed - Mad.

Remuda - A term applied to all of the horses in a particular outfit. Sp. Exchange. Remuda de caballos, relay of horses.

Rig - Saddle.

Right-hand man - Chief foreman of a cattle outfit.

Roll in - To get into one's bed roll to sleep.

Roundup - The gathering of the herd.

Roustabout - A man of all work about a camp.

Running iron - Ring or bar, or even piece of wire or tool used for branding in emergency.

Rustle - To steal cattle.

Savvy - v. To understand.

Sawbones - A doctor named so because he did amputations with a surgical saw.

Seam squirrels - Cooties.

Sioux eye - One blue eye.

Skin mules - To drive mules.

Slow elk - A cow that is stolen and butchered and the meat eaten or sold.

Spurs

Green River skinning knife

Fish or slicker

44 Winchester
(Model 1866 yellow
boy)

Snubbing post - Post around which cowboy takes a 'dally weltie' or hitch to hold animal. Usually in a corral between center and fence.

Sop and hot rocks - Gravy and biscuits.

Sourdough starter - An envelope of yeast, 1 teaspoon sugar, 1 cup warm water and enough flour to make a thin batter. Let stand at room temperature for three to four days until it smells like alcohol or vinegar.

Sow belly - Salt pork.

Spit and vinegar - Full of energy.

Stump sucker - A horse with a vice of biting or getting his teeth against something and sucking wind.

Strays - Estray cattle.

String - Horses assigned each rider.

Sunday hoss - A horse with an easy saddle gait—usually a single footer with some style.

Sunfisher - A horse that darts from one side to another when bucking, giving the effect of switching ends.

Tallow - Fat.

Top hand - A good all-round cowhand.

Two-gun man - One who uses a gun in each hand at the same time. Very scarce, even in the Old West.

Two bits - Twenty-five cents.

Vamoose - To leave in a hurry.

Waddy - In the fall and spring when some ranchers were short-handed, they took on anyone who was able to ride a horse and used him for a day or so; hence the word 'waddy,' derived from wadding — anything to fill in.

Wattle - A dewlap that forms a bunch instead of a string. Made for identification.

Wrangler - One who herds horses.

Yamping - Ordinary stealing.